THE AWAKENING

Jon Evans

Table of Contents

Chapter 1

"It was all a conspiracy?"

Sitting in the back room of our rambler in Tucumcari, New Mexico, my father croaked out choked shouts. My mother and I rushed through the dark hallway connecting the back room to the rest of the house. We sprinted through the kitchen and the hallway where my parent's bedroom lay, into the front room with the 50-inch QLED television. Upon reaching his side, Momma shook my father unsuccessfully averting his attention from the TV. My father, a man of few words and no emotions, could sit and watch that TV for hours without so much as blinking. However, something was different; he was not droning as he usually did when watching the sporting events. No, something latched on to the deepest recesses of his psyche and did not offer him freedom.

Just then, my father's hand rose in response to Momma's prodding, pointing at the TV. We stared at the screen, where an unfamiliar insignia appeared as a circle with an assortment of colors within. The words paraded at the bottom of the screen, *"Aliens are real! President to address nation."* Momma froze in shock, seemingly troubled by the words. I wasn't sure what to do, so I just sat on the floor and crossed my legs. The tune *Hail to the Chief* on the TV broke the silence in the room.

Then the screen faded onto the Oval Office, where a camera was trained on Madam President Tamara Martin, seated at the iconic resolute desk. She sat forward in her chair, gripping her hands together tightly, preparing to declassify the greatest conspiracy known to man.

She said, "My fellow Americans, as many of you have discovered and numerous others will in a few moments, your federal government has betrayed you by keeping and covering up a long-standing secret. I ran my historic 2020 campaign on 'Honesty at all Costs.' At my inauguration two days ago, I promised that I would immediately go to work for the American people. Today, I deliver on that promise." She held up a box full of papers. "These documents outline the discovery, detainment, research, and analysis that occurred at Area 51. Ladies and Gentlemen, we found extraterrestrial life forms from the planet Mars, and they have remained under imprisonment for the past 70 years. It will take time, but I want to assure you we will declassify every single document. The classification review is ongoing with the release of everything set for April 22, 2021, just three months from today. I want to take this moment on behalf of your Federal Government to apologize for this deception and ask you to take time to process how this affects you all. The United States Government will debrief these aliens and provide them with accommodations to resettle in a nearby camp. They will be kept under armed guard until we can negotiate a plan to provide them with a permanent habitation and representation. God Bless America."

And then the news story was over. The television went blank for a moment, and then to an old episode of Star Trek. I remember the irony of the moment as the people who made this probably never knew there were aliens in the universe. My thoughts drifted on the classified documents that would tell us if Martians could harness the technology popularized in the episodes. My father glanced at Momma, grimaced, and then walked out of the house. He did not take anything with him. This man left the house, his car, and his clothes behind.

My mother sat there and passively accepted our reality. I remember chasing after my father when my mother grabbed my arm and sat me down. "No, baby boy, let him go." There was a finality to her words that I could not quite see at the time. A secret they held, untold to the world, that made her understand his departure in a way no one else could see.

Her eyes welled up with tears and she kept a smile on her face as she hugged and kissed me. Her tears conveyed a peace or relief, as if the worst chapter in a book was finished. I sat in my mother's lap and held her for hours that day. She did not say anything for a time, and then she was okay.

The police looked for a short period, but never fully committed to finding him. I even overheard the officers telling Momma we were better without him. No one in town cared or missed my father. Whispers around the community speculated infidelity. Kids were cruel, relaying details of dinnertime conversations about how my father was abusive. Even our church congregation, despite its charity, wasn't immune to the destructive gossip of a community with too little to do. It hurt to hear those things, I never remember him hurting me, nor touching me. My father was not a warm man, but he was not any of those hurtful things that other people said about him.

Later, Momma explained my father's departure by saying he was unable to handle the idea that Aliens exist and probably went off to Tucumcari Mountain to kill himself. I never thought about it much afterwards, but her story was unbelievable. A legend of love and death surrounded our little community, but I doubt my father took his own life.

Regardless, I recognized the truth: he was not coming back. Death or not, that truth hurt me the most.

I only thought about Momma and the events surrounding my father's departure when I was getting ready to discuss my research on the beings from another world. Maybe my research would allow me to connect with my father, since that is the only significant memory I had of him. At that moment, I was thinking of them as I took in a deep breath and I traversed the doors into the vestibule of the prestigious César Estrada Chavez Institute for Social Advancement in Washington D.C.

I mentally prepared myself, as all students do, for the thorough dissection that my person would have to endure. As a Ph.D. student in Philosophical studies, I knew that the usefulness of such studies was sometimes questioned by reasonable minds. This especially became contentious when I proposed performing research on extraterrestrial ethics. No human was interested in bridging the rights gap between humans and these 'Martians,' as well as understand their culture and which lens to view humanity's crime against these beings. Additionally, examining their ethics may give us an idea on how to properly atone for our sins.

However, that contention created a completely new field of study with me as the pioneer, or guinea pig. If I was honest, I knew I could do nothing else. This was my only link to my father and the beginning of a new life with my momma. So, I started a new field to do what I believe humanity should have done years ago to answer for the horrors of our actions at Area 51. This program would award me a contract worth $700,000 over the course of four years, to live, work, purchase supplies, and whatever else needed to make it so that I could focus completely on my work.

"Now, I have come before the board of this institute to garner support for the completion of my research. This is particularly intriguing to me because it will allow me autonomy to develop my ideas and present those ideas to this committee so that I may receive the amount of funding needed to continue my work. Getting this grant would allow me to work for myself, at a pace that is agreed upon by my clients, and build upon ideas that I believe will change the world." The words rattled out of my mouth as Lola Gonzales, the graduate student turned receptionist, sat at a makeshift card table pretending to review some papers. She would take a few papers out of the pile, shuffle them, stack them neatly into another pile, and repeat until the pile was shifted. She would break the monotony by checking her phone until she realized that there was nothing for her and go back to stacking papers.

The student continued to ignore me. "Um, excuse me Lola," I managed to squeak. Lola looked up at me, pressing her glasses from the brim of her nose to her eyes. She looked annoyed, and I lost all my indignation which gave way to timidity. "Are you supposed to do something to get this started? I just want to make sure that there is nothing else that I need to do."

She scoffed a little under her breath. "Everything is ok, sir. Please have a seat."

Realizing I was pacing the room, I sat in the pew near the exit door anticipating what I was going to say, what questions would arise, and how I would address those questions.

Looking around, I noticed what looked like ticket windows neatly stationed to my left that suggested this was converted from an old theatre. I wondered what shows were put on in this building and what famous names must have graced the stage. The carpet was a plain purple with brown walls. The room smelled of Sandalwood-scented candles that barely covered a slight stench of musk. The building must have experienced leaks, and I recalled it raining recently.

I looked down at my brown leather executive satchel, a gift from my maternal grandparents after they passed. The leather was well-worn but high quality, and it remained my default bag for my assorted pencils, papers, and pens. I popped open the clasps and peered into my satchel. The subject of my search, an instruction sheet to reiterate the unchanging requirements for this presentation.

I thought I would be there for five minutes, but it had been ten minutes since I arrived. I looked back at the instruction sheet, which told interviewees to arrive fifteen minutes early. I arrived only five minutes early because I set my alarm for 7 p.m. instead of a.m. A deep regret overtook me as I contemplated the idea they were going to move ahead without me. I was tempted to blame the interviewers for unclear instructions, hunting for mistakes on the instruction sheet. Whatever was triggering my anxiety, I recognized the sign that I over-thinking excuses for my tardiness.

"Vance?" My name was called from the giant wooden doors by a short, white haired man, his voice cracking on the "e." He wore round eyeglasses, a ruffled white shirt, a tan blazer, a pair of green corduroys, and a brown pair of dress shoes. He looked more like the 15th century equivalent of a candy factory owner than he did a representative of one of the most progressive social institutions in the world. I let that thought cause a smirk to creak across my face and walked through the doors into the great hall.

The great hall looked like a very large theatre combined with a church. The rows of seats were set to face the stage, which I assumed was converted from an altar, and there was an area appearing like a retro choir which now housed the board of directors. The echoes of my shoes on the wooden floor as I walked into the room rattled my already weak nerves. The ceiling was hand-painted with the image of the man that inspired the learning in this place. In the mural, his hands were extended to the respective organizations of the people he desired to bridge, the workers and farmers all reached for his hand over the city, and his hand hovered over a government building, hands holding what looked like bills or laws, money, jewels, and other trinkets, which represented the elite institution.

The old man escorted me down the aisle and into the spotlight at the center of the stage. Once I was in place, he whispered, "Good luck," and the old man took his place with the directors. In the spotlight, my vision was not perfect, but I managed to gather there were three individuals sitting in the directors' seats. One was a large middle eastern man, with a great black robe, seated in the middle. The man to his right was a lanky black man, with long and bony fingers, twiddling his thumbs. The third was the old man, a short white-haired man, seated to the left of the middle. The arrangement was such that the middle director was highest, followed by the black man on the right, and the white-haired man on the left. The seated directors looked like they were behind a massive fifteen-foot desk, and they sat glaring at me.

After five seconds of silence, the middle eastern man in the middle said, "Welcome to the institute. I am sure that you understand why you are here and have prepared a suitable presentation for my colleagues and myself. My name is Samuel, the man to my right is Judah, and the man to my left is Ben."

I sat silently and stared into Samuel's eyes. They had a ferocity that suggested he was a stringent man. His words boomed from his voice with authority, much like the sound of lion's roar. In fact, his long, dark brown hair, which was slicked back down to his shoulders, combined with his full beard that stretched down to the middle of his chest, served as a sufficient mane. I listened as he described his expectations for the program and what I was to do for the interview.

"Mr. Vance, as I am sure you are aware, we are the founders of this institute and we created this program to award innovations in social advancement by providing negotiated funding to a post-doctoral researcher without the distraction of a mentor with an agenda. You would be free to research the topic of interest that you will present today and be held solely liable for the success and continued funding of that research. As you have provided a proposal worthy of consideration, we expect that you have prepared yourself to discuss the finer points of what your topic will entail, the sort of work that will be required to get your results, and the need for us to find it rather than approach through a normal graduate study. I offer you a fair warning that your tardiness did not go unnoticed and has significantly set back your consideration. However, because this time is slotted to you, we will allow you to make your presentation. You may begin if you so desire."

I was shocked. So many questions were running through my mind. *Lash out,* my mind demanded. It was as if I could feel the anger boil within the pockets of my soul. I had come so far and spent so many hours on this proposal that I would not be considered. My mind flooded with excuses and arguments of discriminatory practices. The scenarios played out in my mind as Joseph Vance, the victim, argued his plight and blamed the directors for his lateness. *Do it.* I could feel Samuel knew what was on my mind, seemingly baiting me to tell him what I felt.

Then, the whispers of my conscience overtook me: these deep throaty notes that were audibly fighting my anxiety and tendency towards victimhood. After a moment, no excuse felt good enough; I gathered my notes and began.

"Thank you for this opportunity to present before this board. There is no excuse for my lateness and I place myself at the mercy of this board, as you are my only option. All the hope for my life's work and research was placed into this one program. All because no one else is interested in the outcomes from my work." I paused for a second as the board members nodded that they received my message.

"Gentlemen, my name is Joseph Christian Vance and I am proposing that we work together to understand the plight of the Martian being. Too long have we lived with the horrible truth of their misery at our willful hands. These beings furnished the knowledge and the hands that built the innovative products that catapulted American society and the world into what we can agree is the technology age. The technological advances of the telephone, television, and car are a few examples of the byproducts of the research of the aircraft and electronics technology that was transported with the Martians. All of this came against their will and violated basic rights that would have been met with outrage and the possibility of anarchy if done to humans today."

I could tell that the men on the board were intrigued by my declaration. They all leaned forward in their seats. They had their fingers intertwined on the desk and were considering what I was saying. I had practiced Selah, the art of pausing at key points in my discussion, to allow the listeners to ponder a point. I waited a moment longer and then I began again.

"The César Estrada Chavez Institute for Social Advancement is an organization that wants to be at the forefront of the discussion on rights to those who are disenfranchised. Martians represent the ultimate cause, as they are not granted the basic consideration of humanity. They are looked upon as non-persons, or even worse, parasites. Some people literally see Martians as bugs that need to be exterminated. The best that humanity has to offer our guests is hate, disrespect, and enslavement. Martians have a story that needs to be told. I have a contact with the Martians, Delilah Johnson, who has promised me access and information if I can pay my own room and board costs as well as contribute to the upkeep of their central facility in the Washington, DC metropolitan area.

Who really knows how the Martians came to Earth? What happened on their home planet? How long ago did it occur? What do they know about the universe? These are questions that could give us incredible insight into a group of beings that may very well hold valuable lessons from a world they cannot seem to return to now."

Just then, Samuel interrupted me with the raising of his hand. I am not sure why I stopped talking, but it was almost as if my mouth could not make words and my thoughts just ceased. His eyes, I think they had a reddish tint to them, seemed to peer into my soul and demand an account for every word I had just prolifically distorted to my gain. His countenance commanded understanding, and his companions looked upon him in anticipation of what was about to be said.

"Your presentation is well understood, and I agree with the conclusion. However, what makes you think that the scientists at Area 51 did not already complete this research? What makes you think that Martians know more than us? They came to us, and we have enslaved them. Does that not seem odd to you? If they were so strong, could they not have rained destruction on humanity? How do you actually plan to figure out their 'true' purpose if the greatest scientific and analytical minds at Area 51 were unable to do so?"

His voice migrated to my ears and infused with my mind to become my own thoughts. I began to accuse myself for not doing my due diligence. My bias against Martians was brought to my mind and stood judgement for my reasons to help them. Their appearance was marred by the departure of my father. Unable to separate the two, I was unprepared to answer the simplest question. "I am not sure how I will accomplish this task. My contact, Ms. Johnson, did not provide much information and I do not know why she pursued me." I lowered my head, accepting my fate and thinking of the failure I had become.

Another voice started speaking, "Samuel," Judah whispered with a slight African accent. "I believe our candidate has made an admirable proposal considering the frayed relations between Martians and humans. Somehow, he has attained an access to these beings that no other human has garnered. That much should be celebrated. We are an organization that funds novel research ideas, and we love to champion causes of reconciliation. If this man can bridge this gap, let us help him do so."

With that statement, Judah turned his face towards me. He had a warm smile on his face, but I could feel the intensity in his gaze. His eyes were dark and bright at the same time, much like burning coals. Judah's gaze woke a deep fear and touched the core of my soul. I could not look at his face for very long. My eyes watered and my ears started ringing. Judah then said, "I will sponsor him. I will sponsor his research personally and he will report to this committee through me."

My heart stopped beating. I gulped, a heavy lump in my throat. A feeling washed over me that was akin to joy. In the passing of a moment, my research was saved, and it appeared I was going to receive the coveted grant on the spot.

Samuel considered this and looked to me. "Do you agree to these terms? This is a favorable contract to have Judah be your champion. However, I will place Benjamin as the person you will report to directly. He will serve as your champion on the board while Judah sponsors you, and I will evaluate you. We are all available to answer your questions and provide mentorship, should you desire. Congratulations."

The air rushed from my mouth in a gasp of disbelief. I looked on each of the men with a newfound appreciation. Maybe it was the positioning of the lights or an excitement, but I saw these men glowing. The light appeared to emanate from the pores of their skins. I sat in awe, until I realized I was gawking. "I accept," was my sole reply to the board.

Chapter 2

The cool and temperate autumn morning hit my face as I begin my journey to Martian City. I reminisced on my inability to sleep over the past few days, including my last night in the hotel room on the outskirts of Washington DC. Everything that I had to do in the week of preparation to come to the Martian capital was more tedious than I had imagined. I also replayed the interview in my dreams, imagining the directors were listening to me talk, but I could not stay awake. *"What are you doing Vance?"* Their voices kept repeating as I tried to force myself awake to say my speech, only to recite it in my bed towards the ceiling. I shook at the effect that meeting had on me.

The $700,000 check and terms from the board was sent to me in one giant packet, two days after the interview. I did not have much time to prepare for my trip from New Mexico if I wanted to meet their timeline and expectations. My hands rattled while holding the check, hoping that I could keep it just in case the money was reclaimed. Having this much money was scary to me. I knew I wasn't rich; however, I recognized that 700k was more than most people would make in a lifetime. Having it all at one time created feelings and necessitated certain expenditures, yet levied me with a massive burden. The terms of the program were flexible, and reiterated in multiple places that the funds were meant to fulfill my needs—and some wants—so I may focus exclusively on my research. The words on the page echoed in my mind: "The money is yours to use however you discern. Our only requirement is that you solely focus on your research and document your findings providing them to us. Outside of that, we allow you to spend your money however you wish. Be mindful about gaining the whole world and losing your soul in the process." The warning reached from the page and choked my soul, as if the threat were direct and intentional.

I met with many bankers and investment advisers to discuss spending plans and savings options. They bored me with talks of long-term planning while I was thinking about First Class airfare and fancy steak dinners. I ended up creating a conservative annuity that paid out in regular intervals, like a paycheck, around 75,000 a year. With the $50,000 I took out to spend however I liked, I managed to have about 10 years of income stream coming. Despite my newfound wealth, I recognized I was irresponsible, and this money needed to last however long it would take to complete my research and work beyond that. Also, there was the possibility that I may have needed to pay an employee or for more supplies during my research. The 75k covered all my living and business expenses, if none of it was extravagant.

The flight from Albuquerque to Ronald Reagan National was a long day due to a layover, but I enjoyed the first-class accommodations. My financial advisor admonished me for my decision making in not-so-nice terms—"What the hell were you thinking?"—and I hated his response, including my own internal processing of guilt, but I felt I needed the experience. I also arrived at the Nation's capital more rested than I think I would've had I flown coach.

Once I landed, I trekked to my hotel to begin my preparations for my research. From the horizon, the Martian capital looked like a kingdom of sorts, except it was disgusting and dirty. The central castle lacked a tower or even a steeple.

The wall that surrounded the city, keeping the Martians from accessing the human citizens, made the trip from Bowie long and indirect. I used to look at pictures of these colorful slums as a child and imagine a wonderful life for the Martians inside the walls. The red, blue, yellow, and green combination of colors gave a distinct look to the countryside as opposed to the plain colors of the city. However, I noticed there was never any grass in the pictures of the Martian capital as a child.

Oddly, I didn't appreciate how much effort went into keeping Martians away from human contact. Ever since The Great Revelation of extra-terrestrial life in 2021 by President Martin, the relations between the humans and the Martians had been characterized as polarizing. Some humans stood outside the grounds with posters, threatening any Martians that leave with sudden death. Other people set up altars with incense and worshipped the beings for the sky. Most normal people were ambivalent or apathetic. I was undecided as well, but saw an opportunity and took it. People on each extreme reached out to me to congratulate me for gaining admittance and supporting their cause, or to warn me about the imminent judgement from God over me getting too close. I wasn't sure what God thought about the Martians, but I doubted He felt a strong need to judge Martians for being subjected to slavery and an unfair political standing. My tormentors grew out of being minor annoyances to threats when I found dead entrails purposely left in the front yard of my childhood home. I called in police and changed my phone number. Despite my misgivings about the religious zealots, I couldn't help feeling like they were on to something. Martians were difficult for me.

My conflicted feelings about Martians rooted were in my father's departure. The other kids joked about my father leaving, but one kid speculated that my dad probably was a Martian and took off to be with his real family. I fought him a lot, including this one time he called Momma a whore. She never remarried because she devoted herself to my development. However, the backwards minds in my hometown couldn't imagine a single woman being single for the sake of living her life in peace. I remember her always saying, "It's a good thing to be single, Joseph." My momma relished in her freedom from my father and made our home much happier as a result.

Closing in on the checkpoint into the capital, I reflected on the predicament of Martian legality. Martians were not considered a sovereign nation as the Supreme Court defined them, because Martians were viewed as illegal aliens in the most literal terms. I thought it was a bit ironic, since they could not go anywhere. Whatever technology got them to Earth did not seem accessible to get them off. They were in this muddied legal realm between refugees and prisoners. The world's leaders met with the representatives of the Martian community to iron out the details of a deal to gain status and sanctuary. Every nation agreed that the United States should house the Martians since Americans imprisoned them. However, it is rumored that some nations have provided asylum and possibly legal representation to the Martians. Being in America allowed for the Martians to have legal space to live with the headquarters being outside of the political capital of America, Washington, DC. The proximity also allowed for further political negotiations with different levels of fruitfulness, depending on the political party running the government at the time.

My contact, Delilah Johnson, or "Dillie" as she would have me call her, was a part of this movement and helped create the deal that would set aside communities for the Martians to live in to assimilate into human society.

According to Dillie and many other disenfranchised Martians, the assimilation never happened, and the Martians have been living in destitute prisons of communities all over America ever since. However, insensitive studies indicated that many Martians have successfully integrated into society and thrived at the expense of humans in society who have lost out on valuable experience and income due to forced partialism to Martians. They saw the expense of the compound and the development of certain "planned" neighborhoods as gross misuse of taxpayer funds. Not so much of a lie as it was a delusion. My personal position was that Martians were gaining access to improved resources, but progress remained slow.

I reflected on my fortune in being able to come to the twenty-four-acre capital city of the Martians in Bowie, Maryland as a part of my research. With the revelation of the Martian beings and the possibilities of other non-Earth life forms, an interest in extraterrestrial work had sparked a lot of funding and research, but no one ever showed interest in the well-being of the Martians. The work of other researchers mainly focused on improving human technology, but ignored the quality of life for these beings. Looking upon the large, colorful compound, I realized that my plan to definitively answer the questions regarding the reasons Martians do not feel as successful as their human counterparts was a complicated venture. Some humans feel as though they have done things to contribute their failure and the movement to extend their rights was misguided. Others felt like they spent years being behind and therefore do not have a chance to acclimate into human society unless financial concessions were made. Either way, as much as I had been criticized and mentioned on conspiracy and enthusiast blog sites, I was still surprised to the lack of attention my work was receiving. Maybe the whole world knew I would fail. Maybe I felt like this because I knew I would fail.

The security gate around the compound was designed to serve as more of an impermeable membrane to keep humanity out, with no real conviction on keeping Martians inside. It was made apparent with the lack of egress procedures when I told the guards that I was going into the compound. I gritted my teeth as the government contractors fumbled about, trying to set up the scanning equipment to check me before I went in.

Looking at the flying buttresses columns on the wall that surrounded the city, I reminisced over the many times humans had gathered outside these wrought grounds with ambiguous intent, only to be turned away. I inhaled satisfaction for being the only human ever extended an invitation to study the Martian beings.

"Who are you and what are you here for?" The guard pulled out a slip of paper with one name on it, clearly mine.

Annoyed, I spat out, "My name is Joseph Christian Vance and I am here for a meeting with Delilah Johnson." All the sudden, the deafening sound of my own self-doubt came crushing on top of my conscience to reveal to me my true intentions. I shivered as the guard walked me through the metal detector and informed me of my surrendered rights, as I would not be dealing with humans when I crossed the border. I shifted the blame from Delilah to the interviewers at the institute for how I found myself in this predicament. I cursed Momma and my college professors for not preparing me for the realities of life. Just then, I wished I could go back to college and be the star pupil of my favorite professors who covered my faults. My fears were realized in a single moment that I had no plan or any idea as to the goal of accomplishing my project.

Chapter 3

Upon reaching the center of Martian community, I was ambushed by two Martian spawn, a little male who might have been five and a little female who could have been eight. The boy was maybe thirty pounds and stood at two and a half feet. He was average compared to other Martians. His clothes were dirty, maybe due to the recent rain, and it reeked as if he had not had a change of clothes in a long time. The little girl was similar. Her scalp was inflamed, due to a failed hair implant they sometimes undergo. The chemicals may have been overused on her scalp to implant the hair follicles and left her with a raw, bald head. She must have been in a lot of pain, as the infection on her scalp had not been properly treated. They were also wearing signs on their chests to signify that their parents were no longer their keepers. The message was written in English and it requested that the compound have mercy on the children and feed them and clothe them as they saw fit. Martian society was a communal group and did not place heavy emphasis on individual parenting. It would not be surprising to see the sick, elderly, and children abandoned to be cared for by the public in a Martian philosophy. It sickened me to know that Martians probably knew the parents and would not hold them accountable for leaving these children.

The little Martian boy came up to me and held out his hand. His eyes looking at the ground. His right hand was barely at the level of my waist. His four green fingers were slightly bulbous at the end of each digit. I wasn't completely sure if that was a medical condition or not. Martian pathology had not been sufficiently examined to determine if something like this was a problem. The lines in his hand were invisible due to the amount of dirt. He was not wearing a shirt. His pants were too large in the waist, but too short for his legs. These clothes were meant for a husky human youth. He had no socks and red sandals, exposing his five toes. No toenails, just five cylindrical stubs.

His stench attacked my senses further with the smell of urine and a wet dog. I tried to not express my disdain for the child. Did he know what I was doing for their community? If he truly understood what I was trying to accomplish, would he ask for money? The girl stood back, too cautious to approach me. However, her eyes remained fixated on me.

"Young man," I said to him. "What is your name? What do you want?" Masking my disgust was impossible. Even I was a bit surprised by my own disdain for these youths. Something about them made me want to shout, and a strong feeling engulfed me to smack him. It took all I had to resist.

He kept his head down with his eyes to the ground. The little Martian girl who was standing back had took a few steps toward me. Her body had begun to develop, a result of Martian puberty or kaisoisee, one of the few terms in the Martian language that was shared with humanity. A term that was probably created for humans, but offers a glimpse into Martian society nonetheless.

Kaisoisee means a journey to a specified point that every Martian will eventually achieve if given enough time. There is no other way to explain it in human terms, but every Martian gets to a certain point in their lives when they are considered adult. Once at that level, they do not really grow older per se, they just continue to exist until they die. Not many have died from old age yet, and they appear to be able to live a few hundred years at least. If it were not for worry lines and the cracking in older Martian voices, no human would be able to tell a young Martian from an old Martian. Kaisoisee also signifies the age at which a youth would be considered an adult and be responsible for his/her own advancement. If this little girl was entering adulthood, she could still be cared for, but she would be another ice cube in an overflowing cup.

The Martian girl carefully inched closer and closer to me. The color of her eyes was a milky yellow. Her scars came into full view. The patches of baldness on her head looked like several small burns to her scalp. It was as if someone used her head as an ash tray. She was wearing a t-shirt from what I could assume was a rock band, but I did not recognize the group. Her dress was torn to the top of her thigh on the left leg but stretched down to her ankles. She was wearing shoes that were a few sizes too big and caused her to make clunky steps. She stopped right next to the boy and said, "He is too nervous to talk. His name is Bart, and he is blind. I am Esmerelda. You are human." She said it matter-of-factly as if she was trying to convince herself, or possibly narrate for her blind companion. Her voice sounded like a little girl, but she seemed well-spoken for her age.

"Yes, I am. My name is Joseph. I am here to study the Martian's socioeconomic circumstance and observe Martian culture and ethics, all from a philosophical point of view." I straightened my posture and prepared some sort of pose as if to all them to bask in my greatness.

"You are basically here to judge us." She said it flatly without a flinch. Her gaze was unwavering as I darted my eyes, considering the truth behind her statement. She continued on, "You can continue trying to drum up a response. I do not really care one way or another, we are hungry for some sweets and could use a little money. Martians are generous to the poor, but only provide the bare necessities."

"Clever," was the only response I could throw out. This young Martian was good with words and better on her feet. I am sure that the life of an academic would have suited her well. Those two wanted money, and it was for something as frivolous as candy. I hated giving out money, because I did not understand how I could work every day and make a living while beggars had their hands out. Martian society eliminated the need for begging by establishing the communal living situation and providing for the basic needs of all. Humanity still had not figured out the proper balance, so I often looked to the needy as a nuisance. I pulled out a few coins and placed them in the boy's hand to his chagrin. He scowled like he wanted more, but I was already moving by the time the girl finished counting and looked up from their newfound riches.

I walked through the makeshift city in awe of the colors and combination of buildings. The main street had a flair of old and new. The buildings looked like Victorian era homes with grand balconies and slated roofs stacked on top of large windows which bend around the corner. On top of that, the main street had cobblestone roadways and an area with small stands to serve as a market. This area was not frequented by cars as the road was well maintained. The day was still early, so the store owners were the only ones out, cleaning up the sidewalk and windows. They took brief glances towards me before going back to whatever they were doing. I wondered if they would hurt me.

The cobblestones were painted alternating colors of red, blue, green, and yellow. Even the clothes and aprons on the store owners were notable for their assortment of colors. I stopped when I located the donut shop.

Chilppe's Donuts was a favorite brand that was exported to humanity. They were not donuts that most people would usually see; these were the size of donut holes but all white, as if liberally dipped in glaze. The donuts were a perfect spherical, each of them the same size of a small bouncy ball. I never had the pleasure of tasting one of these donuts, but I had heard many people compare these donuts to what was known as Manna in the Bible. I made a mental note to get one before I completed my research and waved at the owner, who seemed confused by my presence in the Martian community.

As I completed my walk down the main street, I finally reached the building housing the Martian affairs. It was a large orange building. I think the best estimates were around 300,000 square feet.

An architectural marvel, yet it seemed so simple. The castle-like structure was erected with ashlar limestone stacked to reach about 150 feet high. In keeping with the concept of old world architecture and modern pieces intertwined, the Martian compound had sliding doors.

I crossed the threshold of the castle doors onto a deep red rug, covering yellow tiles. The walls, except for the blue double doors on the opposite side of the wall, were a green color, almost like the trees of the Amazon rainforest. The relatively small foyer was furnished with a desk that was colored a traditional brown. The receptionist behind the desk was a young Martian female who had not taken her eyes off me since I walked through the door of the facility.

I made my way to the receptionist's desk while she continued typing and staring at me. She finally broke the silence once I got to her desk.

"You must me Mr. Vance. Ms. Johnson is waiting for you in her office." She lifted a piece of paper and handed it to me with instructions on how to get to Ms. Delilah Johnson's office. I looked at the slip and noted that Ms. Johnson was on the sixth floor. I went through the double doors and noticed a great room with the same color scheme as the receptionist room, leading to many other hallways in different directions. I looked ahead to the elevator, which had words in graffiti strewn on the doors saying "peace," and I pressed the orange button. The doors to the elevator opened to reveal a dimly lit cab with marble flooring and orange walls. I pressed the sixth-floor button and made my way up to the office. The elevator doors opened, revealing another labyrinth with high-vaulted ceilings, around 30 feet high with an indirect lighting scheme. The walls were cream colored and the floors had thick blue carpet. I walked straight down the hall and through the giant wooden door with the words inscribed "Dillie's Office, Please Come In."

Chapter 4

I stepped past the wooden doors and through a collection of wet paper hanging from the ceiling to see a frail woman with her back to me in a lotus sitting position, singing words to a song I could not quite recall but sounded a lot like a hymn. Her voice was a shrill raspy sound that was surprisingly comforting as she recited, "And He tells me I am His own; and the joy we share, as we tarry there," in an unrecognizable harmony. Her singing voice was a very high whine, almost like a little girl or a very old, crazy woman. It was alarming to hear for the first time, but I convinced myself that I would enjoy hearing her sing if I was going to put up with it for the next few years. She wore a blue-collared shirt that looked like it was for a large man, the sleeves pulled up, with pink linen pants that were obviously given to her after being worn out, and some yellow slip-on shoes. She continued to sing until I began to speak, and then she raised her hand.

"You know it is not polite to interrupt an old woman," she stated regally as she got up from her seated position, directing me to a stationary chair near the large wooden table. She had a hoarse voice, but it was strong and whistling. She was very tall for a Martian, standing at five foot nine with long arms. Her skin was dark green and slightly brownish. She had larger-than-normal eyes, not large like cartoonish Martian toys from pre-Martian times, but noticeable like any other Martian woman. Her eyes were a dark hazel.

"Sorry," I said, not sure how to respond to her statement because I knew she was not old for a Martian. Dillie had told me earlier that she was 220 years old, 'a little over mid-life for a Martian.' Martians' average life expectancy was supposed to be a few hundred years longer than human life expectancy, although science had never figured out why. Some hypothesized that Martian skin shields their bodies from the radiation of the sun which extends their lives. This may be true, as it was incredibly hard to cut a Martian, and their skin seemed to be a very elastic type of metal.

"That is okay," she said. "You must have a lot of questions for me."

I looked at her again. This time she was staring at me, so I started my interview. "Thank you for your time and consideration," I said, "I want this to be an informal interview, so you are comfortable, and I can report accurate information on the leadership. One of my main missions on behalf of the Chavez Institute is to identify the Martian ethical dichotomy, relate that to any injustice that is perceived by Martians, and provide definitive research on the root cause and possible suggestions to resolve the Martian plight."

Her countenance remained friendly at my remark. I waited for something to change. I knew that Martians hated having the injustice they endured to be referred to as anything less than a crime committed by humans. This was a test, partly a control to set a baseline for her reactions and when she would tell the truth. She did not take the bait, so I would have to try again.

Dillie then looked at me with a slight grin, knowing that I was using a technique to warm her up to topics. "I would like to thank you, sir, for your kindness and consideration of the things that we endure. Your time and your resources will go a long way toward helping raise awareness and providing financial support to our affairs."

I cleared my throat, choosing to ignore what she said. "Dillie, how about we start with you telling me about your life and your background?

Dillie began, "I was born of farmers on Mars. I grew up in a strange intermediate period where we were holding on to hope that we could to stay there forever, but we were technically on our way out, being within a few years of the departure.

My community had a lot of respect for educated beings. Martians do things a little differently from humans in that all Martians are born on the same level and all end up contributing to the greater good of society. We took many tests to determine what we would be good at and that became our lives. There was no hierarchy, per se, so beings lived their lives, contributing to Martian community based on their interests and desires.

The exception to this was the 'Zephnache Chie.' This was a body of beings who governed the three pillars of Martian matters. The first was lore, the beings who researched our history and our beliefs. The second was technology, the beings who researched the benefits of significant innovations. The third was health, the beings who researched mental, physiological, and spiritual means of achieving good health. Each of these pillars were led by a symbolic head who served as the cornerstone to the pillar, the Hughneir. The Hughneirs ultimately reported to the 24 Judges, which was the only job that carried a bloodline with it."

I took notes, but asked her to repeat the words 'Zephnache Chie' and 'hughneir' so I could spell them. They were guttural sounding words that required grunting on my part to repeat them. Hughneir felt weird to say and Dillie appeared amused and a bit surprised at my pronunciation.

She continued, "So, when the tests recognized my competitive intelligence and rationality and offered the opportunity for me to attend schools and receive mentorship as a technology developer, my parents made sure I was prepared to go. Martians are not the type of beings that celebrate frivolous things, but my parents threw a secret small event to commemorate the family achievement, since no one else in our bloodline had done this. They spent all their free time helping me research the different technologies and how they work, just so I could ascend to a Hughneir. They told me that they didn't care about the amount of work that it would add to their day on condition that I gave it everything that I had. I look back and realize what they meant. Martian society supports equity, but really does not invest much into a being if that being does not have a long bloodline in the field. It works in the labor force, as the society requires their work to continue forward. The Zephnache Chie was different; everything we did meant something to the people who lived under our gaze. I immediately picked up on the skills, but the administration would forget me unless I was different. Therefore, I ended up cultivating my talents in agriculture technology, as I wanted to find better ways to farm. Looking back, I think it wasn't the best path for my life, as it was motivated by selfishness, not a Martian quality."

Chapter 5

Dillie and I walked into a large boardroom and sat at the table. The walls were bestowed with a curious combination of orange, green, and blue. It honestly seemed more like a nursery for children than a room where the most important Martian matters were discussed. Despite its choice of color, the decorum was finely appointed with a large and sturdy table, albeit red, and the most comfortable leather chairs that accepted my body's proportions with perfection, in bright blue.

Dillie had noticed my seat at the table and grinned. "Feeling important to the cause, are we?" she asked with a bit of playfulness in her voice, but a tinge of sinister intent, as if I might be a distraction. "I need to be able to stretch out and write things down," I replied facetiously, trying to not ruin the good mood. She offered an inquisitive gaze to me while I laid out my notepad, recorder, pens, and Martian thesaurus in a thought-out pile. It was a force of habit. I needed this order or else I would not be able to focus. Dillie smirked at my musings and proceeded to write on some paper. I was relieved that she did not object to my personal effects, especially my recorder. I did not plan to make any use out of it except to have a record of conversations so that I may go back and document information should their native tongue or other nuisances make it into conversation. That thought reminded me that I knew of a few words, but I had no idea what constituted Martian tongue.

The beings were gathered around the table and the meeting room got quiet in preparation for Dillie to speak, when a Martian female walked in with long black hair, a white blouse, and a black-and-white polka dotted pencil skirt. She was pretty by both human and Martian standards, with mocha green skin. I thought of a dark green chocolate mint when I saw her. Her eyes were a little smaller than other Martians, which helped make her look like more of a person. She wore fake lashes and smelled like a meadow of daffodils. A slim but not starving Martian, she caused me to consider a chapter on interspecies attraction. She walked in with a confidence that suggested she had experienced some success in life. She did not belong in this slum.

I stared in wonder as she sauntered toward me. She looked at me with disgust, and moved to the other side of the table. "Who is he and why is he here?" the feminine Martian asked.

I'm not sure why I experienced that emotion, but her statement rubbed me the wrong way.

"You are welcome to ask me, but angry outbursts are always acceptable when good manners cannot be reached." I heard the hushed snickers around the room, which suggested this Martian was not crossed often.

Dillie looked over to me and then to the other Martian. Her annoyance bled into her response. "Joseph Vance. He is the academic that I told you would begin to cover our movement." Dillie continued on as the feminine being sat there glaring at me. "He is telling a story about the work that goes into this movement, and you should be nice or he may write something about you that everyone already knows." I could see that the last statement from Dillie really got under the being's skin, as the room's hushed chuckles turned to guffawing, but she accepted Dillie's assessment and made it to her seat. "Lily Crocus," the being stated to me as she proceeded to pull out a stack of documents from an expandable folder. "I did not make enough copies, but I see enough empty seats, so you can have one." While taking a copy, I thanked her, feeling terrible for my earlier remark. I watched her for the next few moments as she prepared for the meeting. It seemed as though Lily and Dillie were the two main players in this conversation and everyone else was there to referee.

"Now that Lily is here, let us begin," said Dillie. "I am sure she has a lot she would like to tell us." Dillie proceeded to cover the ongoing business of the Martian community. They discussed different issues, such as Martians who were being disenfranchised by humans. The topic switched to the performance of the Martian students and who would be receiving the scholarships. Then, the Martians finally hit on the budget for candidate support. One thing that I noticed was that Lily had something to say regarding all topics. Without fail, Lily would chime in to ask a question or provide some information that Dillie may not have provided. This seemed to frustrate the meeting members and Dillie to a certain extent. But I enjoyed hearing Lily's voice, and she seemed to have a life in her that went beyond just nodding her head in acceptance of Dillie's statements. Following all the discussion, Dillie asked if anyone had anything that they wanted to discuss with the group.

"I do," said Lily.

The collective sigh in the room made me feel sorry for Lily, but she seemed unaware of the group's disdain for her antics and continued with her speech. Lily started, "I would like to discuss the progress on integration opportunities for Martians in the communities with humans. We are giving too little consideration to the whole populous in favor of Martians who look, act, and think mostly human. This board is dishonest to continue that practice. Real Martians are a spectrum of beings that deserve to be individually considered regardless of where they fall on that spectrum. I have taken the liberty of interviewing Martians that do not fit into the normal mold of who we send to live in human communities but who are upstanding, hardworking, and honest beings who will help to raise awareness and interest in who we are."

The gaze of the room shifted to me as one uncomfortable look after another turned towards me while I was writing. I felt so uncomfortable that I put my pen down. All of this in the first day—I wondered how deep the controversy went.

Dillie remained focused on Lily with a smile, almost a smirk, and said, "Thank you, Lily, but you have once again gone outside of what I assigned for you. We pick the best beings who will provide great representation to humanity for a number of reasons. I understand that this seems wrong to you, but the lists I give you are a carefully crafted selection of beings who represent the best of what Martians can offer. Not only that, they will provide the greatest opportunity for return on the investment. We do not need beings with alternative ways of thinking to go against the concept of advancement in our communities. One day, every Martian will be able to be recognized and appreciated for their differences by humanity, but we are better off having the highest quality examples sent off to the human areas. Unless, of course, you have a plan to get us off Earth and make Mars habitable."

"You are wrong, Dillie!" Lily exclaimed, "We do not tell anyone about this program, they do not even know that it is available to them! When I interviewed the artists and the thinkers, they revealed a perspective that we never considered. One of the artists talked about our baldness and how showing the humans how we look in reality could be a difference that we celebrate."

The irony in her statement almost caused me to burst in laughter, but I managed to squawk out a cough as no one else laughed. She had hair on her head, and obviously they were human hair implants. How could she say anything? The room once again fell quiet and all eyes on me. Embarrassed, I broke out into a fake coughing fit and asked for some water to which Dillie obliged. We sat in silence as I sipped water to feel better.

When I gave the thumbs up, Lily continued. "Imagine a human being able to joke about our green skin and lack of hair and we could joke about their spherical heads and their high stature. Imagine celebrating the differences between us in community with no genuine hatred for the other existing. Imagine that Area 51 is scrutinized and humans accept their fault in that happening and teach our children alongside one another the truth about what happened, why it happened, and how progress is a continuing process. Imagine little Martian children living what they see in the mirror without having to go to extreme lengths just to look human. Imagine the Martians not being treated like animals when around humans. And yes, I said animals. The horrible sporting events that serve as the only way for disenfranchised Martians to succeed is just one example of why humans do not respect us. We viciously destroy one another in these sports only to get paid millions to limp away 5 years later. They give us signals and whistles to complete the experience. We are their dogs. Dillie, let's open the process up to all Martians. Being separate from human society is not the end goal; we want the world to acknowledge that we have a place here as well, and peacefully coexist with us in it."

I was not sure what look I was giving Lily, but it must have been stunned, because she fell quiet and did not say anymore. I did not know if I have ever heard it so eloquently put, but Lily's argument made sense. Maybe the approach of taking the best that the Martians had to offer fit into the human model, but did not give way to awareness and tolerance. The humans would never get to see the real Martians and could never accept them. It made perfect sense to me.

I sensed Dillie could read my thoughts and she quickly rebutted this sentiment. "You may not believe this when I tell you, but there is a process and an order to making these things happen. We have a community of people to feed, not just here, but all over the world. You cannot just go and change humanity's minds by expressing sentiment and raising awareness. Humans are desperately stubborn and alarmingly dense. They hate change and they hate things that they do not understand. If we force this change down their throat, especially when this is not our home, we will lose them. We have to take the high road, as we are their guests, and we have to live in their world on their terms until we can truly gain equal footing. Martians were held captive for hundreds of years before humans even acknowledged our existence, and it could take thousands of years to undo that harm. Until then, we paint a picture that will help us get what we need because we have hungry children today. And Lily, another thing, if it wasn't for those 'animals' that you look down upon in the games who are funneling money into the Martian communities, we would not have the advancements in education that we have today. Meeting adjourned."

Dillie's face was calm. Lily was enraged by this comment. She raised her voice, irritated. "I have not finished going over my concerns. Beyond the games, medical researchers have many Martians showing signs of a similar strand of virus, which suggests contagion. It has not reached epidemic proportions but we have more cases that what is being reported and it seems to be spreading faster than our physicians can track it. What are we doing about it?"

Dillie remain unfazed by Lily's comment. "Thank you, Lily, for that education. We are all aware of the sickness that has plagued a small fraction of Martians. If there is a problem, I am sure the physicians will reach out to me. We are all dismissed."

"Shiepol."

I thought I misheard her. It sounded like a groan from deep inside. It was barely audible. I felt like I missed something, but I did not react to the word, out of politeness and confusion.

The room grew quiet. I could see the embarrassment in the faces of the beings in the room. Even Dillie had signs of embarrassment.

"Lily, enough!" A strong show of emotion from Dillie. I wondered if I should have turned off my recorder. Dillie motioned her hands, shooing the other members out of their chairs towards the exit. Lily picked up her effects and left without a word. Dillie looked at me and smiled. "We never have a quick meeting with Lily around. She is kind of a busy body, but she keeps me sharp. I wish I could trust her to follow directions instead of her own value system; she would make one hell of an advocate for the community."

With that, Dillie escorted me to the dinner hall to gather some food. Nothing looked appetizing, but I grabbed what I thought was fruit and sat with Dillie. I started another round of questions.

"You talk about being a champion to the cause in the community, so why is Lily not taken with greater seriousness?"

Dillie replied, "She is taken seriously, but you have to understand my predicament. My job is to negotiate with politicians, businesses, and charitable organizations to provide jobs, food, shelter, and safety to all Martians. This program is a small part of the equation, and does not meet the needs of Martians today. Yes, it would be great to bring about evolutionary change and not have the conversations that we have on a regular basis. However, that is not the priority. If she would meet me halfway and do what I am asking her to do, then I could put more emphasis on her pet projects, but she is an 'all or nothing' type of gal and has never been good with compromise."

I understood her meaning. Dillie was the spokesperson for the Martian community as a whole. To take up Lily's cause would not be the most financially responsible thing to do if the motivation was making sure they had enough money to meet the needs of their constituents. I could not fault her for that, but Lily made such a compelling argument that it would be surprising to hear that she was not placed in charge of a committee for this exact purpose. Walking back to my room, I noticed the beauty of the building, but also how I was never really left alone. Someone was always watching. I traversed into my room, fell onto my bed, and slipped into slumber.

Chapter 6

I awoke to Lily shaking me. I sleepily rubbed the crust out of my eyes before I realized who was standing over me. Why was she in my room? Her hazel eyes seemed to glisten in the dark. She was wearing a long, sheer pink robe with star shaped patterns on the breast and shoulders. I was certain she lacked underclothes. I leaned my head back, groaning, and focused my eyes on her face.

"Sorry to intrude at this time of night," Lily began, looking at the floor and twiddling her fingers. "I did not know if we would have another opportunity to do something like this." She paused as she bit her lip a little.

I was floored. What was I to do? I mean, it was obvious, maybe my musings were inappropriate, but I felt like we shared a moment. She was beautiful. What should I have said? I did not think that I was ready for something like this. Was my hesitation bad? I never considered a Martian female before. It was not common. Was I attracted to her?

I managed to slip out, "I can't do this." That was when I realized I was an idiot.

She looked at me puzzled. She said, "Is this a bad time for an interview? I am really bad at reading situations. I wanted to get my ideas out and I think you would provide a good platform. I also do not sleep much these days."

It dawned on me that she was oblivious to the situation and what I assumed. I wondered if I should say anything. She was attractive. I mean, really attractive. She was the type of attractive that made me question how I view attraction. Her skin was such a perfect shade of green. She did not look rusty, like other Martians, she was the type of green that feels like the Amazonian jungle. And she smelled like berries. I knew nothing about her. I needed to say something, and it would be easier to say something before things got complicated. Besides, she was the subject of a study, and it would be in bad form to pursue such interests with my work at stake. Was my career worth her? I thought I was ahead of myself. I was assuming that she liked me. I assumed that my feelings were sorted and I had real feelings her. But I should probably have answered her question.

"Of course, we can," I responded. "I just need a second to gather my thoughts."

I pulled out my recorder and started the interview. "This is a record of the statement of Lily Crocus for preliminary study. Do you consent to an interview and can you begin by discussing your background?"

Lily sighed and spoke. "I am a researcher of physical and psychological statistics for Martian rights. I analyze quantitative and qualitative data points to help make conclusions about the effect certain things have on Martians. I also provide input on ways to improve human and Martian relations. I have multiple degree in American civics, philosophy, and mathematics from the Hubble Institute of Technology. I received a fellowship through the early education program for Martians and financed my educational pursuits for my life through the program. I grew up in a middle-class home and my parents were both blue collar workers. We were very fortunate, not many Martians had jobs thirty years ago, and not many Martians had good jobs that could support our lifestyle. My parents made a lot of sacrifices so we would not be limited later in life. I graduated college in hopes of pursuing a career in a corporate office. One day, I was giving a presentation where one of the humans asked if my work represented my own analysis or had I stolen someone else's work. This human had no basis to suggest it and could not furnish any reasonable evidence of such infringement. However, the university opened up an investigation on the originality of my work and held the issuance of my diploma until they could prove that I was the originator of the work. I spent 3 years fighting for my work to be recognized and attributed to me. Meanwhile, scores of humans went through the program with less rigor and integrity. In their self-righteousness, many human students would berate me for not being focused enough and criticized that I just needed to stand my ground. I used to get so frustrated when I heard people say that. However, it soon dawned on me, I was perceived as being less than even though it was clear my work was better. And the humans could not understand that it was not fair to consider my work as plagiarism if it was not considered equally across the spectrum.

"I decided from that moment on that I would not allow other Martians to experience that pain. I tried to stop the oppression and attacked the way the institution worked. What if I came to the Martian neighborhoods and gave them the tools to succeed? I was intelligent, and I am sure I could instill that in the younger generation. I originally came to the slums to teach and prepare young Martian students for success, but soon realized that the resources available to prepare Martian youth to succeed were inequitable compared to human resources. After that, I started lobbying for reform. So, I went to Capitol Hill and eventually earned a position as a representative for Martian Advancement. Unfortunately, my work was frequently subverted by my human counterparts to the point that I decided to quit politics and move to activism. I wanted to make a difference. I can add value to the world through my understanding of the struggle. I lack the political prowess and relationships on Capitol Hill that proved useful, but I am working to raise awareness of Martian issues and build public sentiment in favor of Martian rights."

I offered agreement. "That's a great start Lily. It seems like your struggles and the lessons you have learned will provide a framework to assist other Martians on their path to success. What do you think about the Martians who live in the slums who may not have the opportunities that are available to you? You experienced one situation where you were discriminated against, but you still had the opportunity available to you for success. How can you relate to their struggle?"

Lily again took a measured breath. She seemed to struggle with her response as she sat for a second to ponder.

"Some say that I am not personable, and could not possibly relate to the Martian struggle because of my success and upbringing in a middle-class home. They think my life is so privileged that the poorer Martians will have no way to relate to me. They assume I will look at their shortcomings and tell them that they need to do better. They assume the fellowship meant that life was always easy for me. That is not true. Imagine carrying the success of your species on your shoulder. Imagine being hated by every spectrum of beings. The humans hated me because I defied what they assumed to be true about Martians. The Martians hated me because I forced them to recognize that success is possible and nothing to be embarrassed about. The leadership hates me because I have new ideas that challenge the old way of thinking. The public hates me because I am not doing enough to convince the leadership of change.

"Look, I went to Martian schools, but also went to after-school tutoring to improve my grades and test scores. I worked for everything that I have today. I was focused from the first day I entered my courses. I studied everything I could get my hands on and I researched enough topics to be a resource to my fellow beings during the Martian struggle. I ask a lot of questions because I am truly interested in helping Martians. This has not translated into much in the way of results to the Martians, as the work is ongoing. They have expressed frustration in my lack of deliverable results, but I feel overextended in all the work that needs to be done. A better union between Dillie and me would improve results, but cannot be a substitute for the average Martian raising the bar on their success."

I stared intently at her for a moment. I sensed conviction in her voice. She really believed in what she was saying. This sort of determination was infectious. She could be the difference. "You and Dillie had a contentious discussion today," I said. "What was your perspective on why Dillie has a problem with this?"

Lily appeared embarrassed, but leaned closer to my bed. She offered her response in a hushed murmur, as if there were microphones in the room. "Dillie is from a different generation of Martians. They always believed in not stirring the pot more than was necessary. I think it is because they were slaves, and slavery is now their mentality. She thinks that humans are incapable of accepting Martian acclimation into human society. She wants to change perspective over the course of generations, slowly eradicating the hate each turn of a decade. Or maybe, she is hoping for the ability to return back home. I just don't believe in that. She is guilty of doing to humans what they are doing to us. Making assumptions about who they are and interacting with them based on that reasoning. I think Dillie despises humanity on some level because of the pain of the bunkers in Area 51. She is not far removed from the hatred that the Martians had for humans because of the miscarriage of justice. I am not encumbered by that same hatred. I know what happened to us, but I know that generation of humans was a different one. I want us to integrate into society, and I am trusting the humans to help us do just that. I believe that the public is reasonable enough to make an informed decision if they know all the facts. Start integrating all types of Martians into different communities with humans, and I believe that perspectives will change. Imagine how much better it would be than just surprising humanity with the differences between Martians when they have been used to one type that was eerily like them."

"Well, I think we have enough for now, Lily," I said. "I should take some time and think about what has been said. Besides, I think it will give me some time to think of questions that are pertinent to the movement. I want to know the real you and how you fit into the equation. Hey, before you go, what did you mean when you said 'shiepol'? I have never heard that term before."

Lily's eyes widen at my question. She said, "I do not know if we should talk about it." Then she pondered for another few moments. "But maybe we should talk about it over dinner tomorrow. Is that okay, and can you keep this between us?"

I said, "Yes."

With that, she was gone.

I admired Lily for her brevity and respect for humanity. She seemed to trust the ultimate good in humanity and I could not help but feel frustration at how she had been portrayed as this pro-Martian, forget-humanity type of activist. She saw us as educated and reasonable beings who could help Martians assimilate into society if we were given the opportunity to see Martians as they are. However, I could not help but feel that I was missing out on something. Why did we need to discuss her word tomorrow? Was this something more? Why all the secrecy? I fell back into a deep slumber, searching for an answer.

Chapter 7

I awoke the next morning to a commotion outside of my room. It sounded like someone had fallen down. I did not know if it was the nightmares or my lack of sleep, but I sprang into action to distract my mind. Opening the door, I almost stepped on Dillie. She let out a yelp at the sight of me and I reeled back in terror, falling over the clothes I had scattered in my room. Dillie lifted her frail frame enough to stand and walked inside.

The shrill of her voice shattered my tired ears as she spoke. "Well, you aren't one for cleanliness. I'm sure your mother would be proud." With that assessment, Dillie let out a hearty laugh that lasted just a half second too long. I knew she was baiting me to chat further, and I was not in the mood. I was certain she wanted to know something and was working an angle for me to reveal it. Lily had kept me up part of the night allowing me to ask questions that would provide some context into why this work was so important to her. I still did not understand how a bright and ambitious Martian as herself could so foolishly end up in politics, even if it was for fairness and equality. There were so many other ways to make a difference. She could have gotten a high paying job somewhere and sent money back, or become a lobbyist for Martian rights. Instead, she was hidden away in the Martian compound, determining trivial things such as who gets what and how much of it. I also considered the confusion in my mind regarding her interest. She was beautiful, but I was not sure that my attraction to her was romantic or mutual. I did not know much about Lily, but I knew that she loved the

Martian beings. I also did not know about my interests. I never had a desire for companionship and I did not feel like I needed that sort of distraction. I tried to remind myself that this was research, and that had to be my focus. My professors would have berated my already-unfocused mind. I needed to get to work.

Dillie snapped her fingers a few times as I woke up from my musings. I knew that she had a lot planned for me if she was going out of her way to get me out of bed. "Are you ready for breakfast?"

"Yes, Dillie, I need a minute to gather my thoughts and clothing."

Dillie cheered, "Wonderful, I will be outside your door."

I looked for some nice pants and a button up shirt, but settled for some faded, worn, dark denim jeans and a wrinkled t-shirt.

Dillie looked me up and down as I came out the door. She was amused by my choice of attire. "Ah, the classic look of the scholar. Very fitting indeed, sir." She turned, and we started towards the cafeteria as I considered if I really wanted to respond to her sarcasm.

As we were walking, I noticed that the corridor to the cafe looked like a tunnel with graffiti strewn about on the walls. The only difference was it seemed to have a certain order to it. The words all came together to a single theme: War. There was a drawing of two video game fighters, except one was Martian and the other human. In another place, a drawing of American soldiers with a large American flag going over a hill only to find a flying saucer in the horizon. It was sobering to see that the Martians expression was so resistant to humans. I looked over to Dillie as she was humming to herself that same song I heard when I first arrived. She seemed happy, even with all of this discontentment. I wondered what life was like for her in those bunkers.

Dillie interrupted my musings by saying, "Here we are!"

The Martian café looked like a giant hall with a stage. The construction was minimal, as the interior building walls had concrete blocks with a coat of assorted paint colors on top. In true Martian fashion, the room looked like someone had vomited crayon colors all over the walls. The cafeteria had a number of food stations around, and the fare had an international flair to it. I gravitated towards the pastry station. I heard Martian donuts were unrivaled by any other food item on Earth. I picked up the donut with tongs and placed it on my plate. It was a traditional type of donut that was perfectly circular. It had a light brown color and a healthy amount of glaze that seemed firm and even. I could not stop myself; I took a bite. The dough was perfectly fried, which I could tell in the perfect amount of crunch. It was not hard, but it was not chewy. The donut was so light and feathery that I stared in awe for a few moments as my mind wandered to the possibilities of these if mass produced for humans to eat. I needed coffee to enjoy this completely.

I walked with my tray to the coffee station and poured a cup of decaf coffee. As I was admiring the aroma of the freshly ground beans, I felt a tap on my shoulder. I turned, and Dillie was looking at me with a giant smile.

"Let me guess," Dillie began with a face of deductive reasoning, similar to Sherlock Holmes. "You are a caffeine addict and this is the only way you can get your coffee fix and not end up with jittery fingers?"

"I stopped consuming so much caffeine a while back, but I needed this if I was going to eat a donut." I felt a little self-conscious as I looked over my hands for any sign of shaking.

"Ah, the fabled Martian donut. Almost as good as the manna from heaven! Come and sit, Joseph, over there with Lily!" Dillie offered a wicked grin and a drawn-out finger, directing my eyes to Lily.

I froze. Lily was sitting at a table near the middle of the cafe. She was wearing a red tank top with some blue sweatpants. Her hair was tied up and neatly set in a bun over her head. She was wear some reading glasses that could have come from the 1960s. She was astonishingly beautiful. I put one foot in front of the other as I made my way to the table. When I made it to the table, Lily looked up and smiled at me. My soul leapt for joy.

I said, "Good morning Lily, thank you for your insightful remarks."

She looked up at me and said, "What do you mean?"

As Dillie joined us at the table, she said "Oh, he is just talking about the late-night tryst you had with him last night. You know, where you were fraternizing and sneaking around in a human's room to try to understand reproduction."

Lily's face turned red with embarrassment as she began to explain herself. "I most certainly did not. We were simply talking about the struggle, and I am not the type of person to have Joseph..."

Dillie held up her hand and said "You do not have to explain it to me, I am not your God, Lily. Whether or not you did anything with him is beside the point, although that pink getup would have caused a drowning man to walk on water." Just then, she turned to me with a wicked smile. "You did like it, didn't you Joe? The sheer pink lingerie that hugged her curves just right, the sound of her voice as she told you about her life. I am sure it was more than a dark, handsome man such as yourself could handle. Did you at least think about it? No one could fault you."

Lily slapped her hands on the table and said, "Stop Dillie, this is inappropriate."

The room got quiet as all the attention focused on us. Lily's face was flushed, and then she gathered her things. "I feel that it is now time for me to leave Dillie. There must be things that I can attend to now."

With that, Lily stood and left. I looked over at Dillie, who seemed fairly pleased with herself. It was a smug look, like Dillie had just revealed something about Lily's character to the room of spectators.

Something about these interactions bothered me. Why was Lily so annoyed by Dillie? They were in the business of helping their fellow beings. They both wanted the same things. They had two different approaches, but that should not have mattered, right? Dillie was staring intently at me again.

"Where does your mind go?" Dillie began. "You want to ask me a question. What is your question?"

I looked for a moment longer into the blankness of the far wall. So many questions, but none of them material to my paper. Exposing problems within the rankings of their cause could prove troublesome to the Martians. I was not a journalist, but an academic. My only concern was to understand the fundamental thought behind the Martian push for equality. That realization could not stifle my curiosity.

"Dillie," I started, "you and Lily seem to be at odds with one another. How does it benefit you to taunt her in the manner that you do?"

The question appeared to catch Dillie off guard. She looked hurt by my question if only for a second. She curled her lips and spoke. "Everything that I do for Lily is for her benefit. She wants to be a leader for the Martian people, and I honestly believe that she is the one person who is qualified to take my mantle and handle the responsibility of the job one day. She cares about Martians, like genuinely cares about equality. She believes that there is some equality to be gained and we have not brought this on ourselves. Also, Lily could have very well gone and made a name for herself, made a lot of money, and just cut a few checks for us. She did not, she wanted to make a difference by lending her mind and her time. Time is the most valuable commodity, it is the only thing that we cannot make more of in this universe. Every being is limited by the amount of time in its life cycle, we are no different."

She paused for a moment and looked at me. Her big brown eyes seemed more pronounced now. I could tell that she was considering what she said next very carefully. I waited for her to speak.

"Being the leader of a movement means dealing with beings and circumstances that may not make sense unless you know the context. Lily is very smart, but she is not patient with unfavorable situations. If she gets uncomfortable, she becomes defensive, bordering on belligerent. A successful leader has to be consistent when everything and everyone around her is inconsistent. It is a very simple, but difficult principle. Lily is supposed to be the example, she must rise above the difficulties of the world and be whatever her people need her to be. For example, a Martian boy was killed by a human in a shooting incident because he was walking around a neighborhood that does not get very much Martian traffic. The human knew that some people are scared of Martians and decided to give him chase. The human called the police, who told him to wait for officers to arrive and not to engage the being. The human refused, chased the Martian down, and shot him following a fight. Remember? The Martians and sympathizers erupted in protests and solidarity. However, it shifted to violence. Martians versus humans. Lily wanted to go out and join the fray. She believed that standing with our fellow beings was the only response. She was correct in that regard. Standing with our fellow beings would have been a great show of solidarity and be an excellent way to connect to our base. Unfortunately, sentiment does not hold up in the court of rationality. The overall objective does not allow us to react the way our fellow beings react. It is not a condemnation of their actions, but a distinction that we are the leadership. The Martian public's actions are the result of years of anger and pain. As the leadership, we have the job of giving the anger and pain a voice. Participating with the masses does not distinguish us and makes both the humans and apathetic Martians less inclined to listen." Dillie stopped speaking and stared at me for a reaction.

I could not help but feel skeptical about her statement. Dillie did not believe it herself. She looked worn from all the years of politics and suffering. She had seen the worst that the world had to offer. She lived through the enslavement of Area 51. She negotiated the deals that paved the way for Martians to receive land and legal representation on limited issues. She also worked to raise awareness of the horrible injustice that the Martians were forced to endure and continue to face today. She did not get to know what it was like to enjoy an easy life. She would always have to fight until the day she gave up or died.

"I don't believe you," I began. "You want Lily to take over. She has real conviction and would not toe a party line. I think you would take anyone who would be willing to take the unpopular choice and be in the fray. You believe in what you are doing, but the politics is starting to stress you out. You are tired, hurting, and filled with regret. Why?"

Dillie smiled that wicked smile again. "I have not underestimated you, Mr. Vance. Your discernment is keen. I hope you are prepared to use that discernment in the near future."

I did not know what that meant, and I was not interested in finding out. Dillie spoke vaguely to fish information out of me, but I was not one to fall into her trap. She was skilled in communication and probably would have made a good interrogator as a profession. Dillie stared at me for a moment longer and then proceeded to exit the cafeteria.

I followed her out, but could not find her. She somehow had disappeared, and I was left to my own devices. I wondered if she only woke me up this early to show me how she dealt with Lily. Regardless, I decided to carry on with the day.

I spent most of the day walking through the harrowed halls of the Martian capital building and asking questions. Most of the beings doing business in the building seemed dissatisfied with the current state of affairs, but were overall hopeful for the success of future generations of Martians on the Earth. A number openly and bluntly expressed anger with the human's treatment of Martians in society considering the atrocities at Area 51. I figured as much, but it was still surprising to hear that Martians did not feel welcome in human society. So many Martians told me that they felt like their fellow beings who insisted on being true to the identity of a Martian were undermining the progress that was being made. I trudged through the day, anticipating my date with Lily.

Chapter 8

A knock at my door startled me from my sleep. "Yes?" I asked hesitantly, uninterested in being bothered unless it was Lily.

"Are you ready?" Lily's voice came through the barrier. "I can come back if not. Do you require more maintenance?"

"No. I am coming out." I chuckled to myself at the use of the word maintenance when I joined her in the hall. She smiled at me, maybe not realizing I was laughing at her.

She started walking and I followed along with her. I struggled to know how to walk with her. At certain points during our walk, we touched shoulders and I felt chills in my spine.

We left the compound and walked into a nearby diner. "Are you sure it is okay for us to be here?" I looked around to a handful of people scattered throughout the diner minding their own businesses. Most of the people in this place seemed like they were the type of people who would not be eager to be around if I was in the city. They appeared a little rough and probably too poor to live in better neighborhoods, hence they were dining, and probably living, near the US Martian compound.

"It is fine." Lily confidently walked in and guided us towards a booth in the back of the restaurant. "I regularly come to this place and they take any business. Besides, the police have not set up checkpoints since this is a bit of a crime-riddled area and adjacent to the Martian community."

We sat at a booth table and looked over the menu. Lily decided to order some steel cut oatmeal with an assortment of cut fruit and honey. I settled on a steak sandwich with cheddar cheese.

"Okay Joseph, enough with the theatrics," Lily's look at me caused me to experience a feeling similar to fear. "I need you to tell me the truth."

I nervously picked up my cup of water and began to gulp down large swaths. "I am so sorry Lily, I should have been honest during our first conversation. I was not sure if you felt it too. I wondered if this was going to be our first date. I thought I felt something, it feels good to know you saw it too."

"What?" Lily's face expressed confusion. "You thought this was a date? Like we were considering a romantic union?"

My heart dropped. I had never been more humiliated and exposed in my life. I wanted to get up and leave the restaurant. Why was I attracted to a Martian? I had never been attracted to anyone. I raced through thoughts trying to come up with an explanation for my delusions.

Lily reached across the table and touched my shoulder. It broke my thought process. "Joseph, please do not take this the wrong way, but I have not considered anything like that with you. I wanted to know why you are here with the Martians. What do you and Dillie have planned?" She then did something a little startling. She started this deep guttural groaning. "Ei mie ke lo pama kaiah?" She looked at me.

"What does that mean? E meh key loe pamana kai?" I felt the groaning deep inside of my being. It was as if the words came from my soul and exhaled themselves as grunts. It burned in my chest when repeating her words.

Her eyes widen and she almost jumped out of her seat. "Primitive. But you can speak it? What are you?"

"I do not understand the question Lily." I felt confused and lacked an explanation for my skill. "I have always been able to grunt out words."

"But no one else could hear it?" She shot the question as my mind jump towards that thought.

"Yes," I said. "I could never explain the sound, but I used to tell my mom that I could feel myself say it like the feeling of hearing speech in the form of light vibrations." I allowed myself to experience a moment of anticipation. I had not given my skill that much thought over time because I rarely used it. Maybe I had stumbled upon the key to communication with Martians in their native tongue.

"Tell me the truth. What are you and Dillie planning? Is this sabotage? How did she give you the ability to talk our language? I suspected saboteur, but I never expected it to be at this level! This will cost both of you greatly!" She started groaning and grunting, her disappointment was clear.

I was floored. "What have I stumbled into here, Lily?" Planning something with Dillie and sabotage? I feared for my life at that moment. I wondered if she wanted to kill me. She looked that disturbed and I knew how the Martians were about morality. If I am suspected of sabotage, that means I am guilty of one of the greatest forms of a lie.

"Lily, please," I begged her. "Please show me some mercy. I swear on my very existence that I am not hiding anything from you. My word is true and I would suffer torture to prove such." I do not know what went through me, but I bowed my head for her mercy. I knew at that moment that I needed Lily to trust me. Her dedication to the truth and her reaction at the thought of my dishonesty raised my interest in her believing me.

She sat back, unsatisfied with my expression. "I have to be honest. I do not think I should believe you, but I believe you anyway. It may be that I do not trust Dillie more and I could use an ally."

"I can accept that." I knew this would be difficult, but I wanted to help her. Lily was being vulnerable; something Dillie did not offer, and something that I had not experienced from anyone else in my life. It felt good to know that it was all out there. I needed to give her what she needed from me.

"What do you want to know? I will tell you everything I can."

We talked for hours in the diner. It felt like a veil was being lifted and two friends were connecting. I confessed to things that I had not discussed in years just to lay it all out for Lily. She asked me intrusive questions about how I came to know Dillie and what our conversations were like. I talked about our first phone calls and how mysterious it all seemed. I observed how Dillie would groan out words slightly and when pressed, she would say that I must be mistaken because she did not say anything. She asked me about my impressions of Dillie and whether Dillie was planting me as a romantic interest for Lily. I told her about how I did not feel like Dillie was the type of being to offer full disclosure unless it benefitted her. I liked that Lily listened and did not react negatively or positively to what I was saying. It felt good to honestly assess Dillie and the things around me with discernment.

"Look how much time has passed, Lily." I looked at her and she was sipping her coffee and enjoying the moment, I surmised. She smiled and looked out the window. I thought about how our time together may look. "We should probably head back soon, I am sure people are getting suspicious."

"Do not worry about it," Lily shrugged. "Martians are not suspicious beings. We assume the best out of each other, and that trust is what makes us better than humans."

I was a little offended. "Better than humans? How can you say that when you are the ones that have come to our planet?" I wanted to say more, I needed to say more, but those words that came out of my mouth were strong enough.

Lily sipped her coffee again as she stared at me. "Now that is a good question Joseph. I appreciate your frankness, but who are you to judge our reasons for leaving our home planet? Even if we are not better than humans for destroying our own planet, humans lowered the bar when you enslaved us. Despite us coming in peace, we were met with hostility and enslavement. Humans are the true monsters. Guests show up to Earth with nothing and humanity tries break them. Even now, we hold no harshness of perspective against humans. Deep down, we know why you feel this way. Fallen creatures always feel that way."

Her words cut through me like a flaming knife. Even in talking with Martians, there never seemed to be any real animosity against humanity. Martians were angry at the circumstances but did not express hostility towards humans. Humans were the ones who lack civility. Maybe they viewed us as nothing more than animals with instincts. Maybe, in our 'fallen' state, we lacked the capacity to see beyond our rock and care for outsiders. I shivered with frustration inside at the prospect that we were not meeting the standard of morality in the greater universe. What if there are other beings watching us from afar who would not like what one would see out of humans when it comes to the treatment of Martians. How did we 'fall'? Were we still 'falling'? The question annoyed me. I wanted to ask something profound, but I felt my lack of experience showing and I needed to know. "Lily, how would you know how a human feels?"

She sighed and looked at me as if she was explaining bad news to a child. "This universe is more connected than you can imagine. We have a knowledge that is beyond human capacity and it would undermine your understanding of your entire existence if you could comprehend it."

I wanted to know more. I felt my heart beginning to race in anticipation as to what she may reveal. "Like what?"

"Joseph, maybe another day. The deep truths of this universe are not easy or short conversations. You would need to be able to comprehend the Martian tongue. Because you can understand the words of a Martian; unlike other humans, you may yet be able to seek out those deeper truths. If you are in fact useful, I may confess to you my real name."

With that statement, Lily grabbed my hands in hers and held them there for a few moments. She looked at me, a look that I assumed would be reserved for a date that went well. I felt a strong urge to squeeze her hands. A strong attraction for her grew in my heart. I had not known her very long, but I felt like we knew each other. I bared my soul to her and she unleashed her doubts to me. Was this our moment? I was nervous as to what I would say in response to the soliloquy she would present to me in a few moments.

"Joseph," she said to me in a yearning voice. "Thank you for caring enough about the Martians to not betray our cause. I know Dillie is plotting something, but I have to ask you to allow her to continue on her path and report to me her goings. Also, keep your knowledge of our language to yourself. I do not want her plan to be activated or concealed before she can be properly exposed. I love my fellow beings and I would give my life for their safety. You have given me hope that the greater Martian good will prevail. Thank you again Joseph. Oh, by the way, 'shiepol' means rude or aggressive person. Never repeat it."

I was flattered by her sentiment. I bowed my head and looked at the table. I think her admiration for me had touched something inside of me more than all the acts of love. "Thank you, Lily, I did nothing but ask a question and you opened the door for all of this. I have never been able to open up on this level before. You have made my heart truly care for the Martians. I will work to understand your language so your traditions may be based on more than observation to me. You also are a wonderful being whose selflessness deserves to be emulated by everyone who calls themselves leaders. I look forward to knowing your true name."

She blushed, and I felt a strong wave flow through my hand and spread throughout my body like a chill that shook me violently. She began to form a tear and reached her hands to her face and wiped it.

"Okay, I think we have stayed out too late. Let us go back before there are questions about what we are doing."

As we were getting up from the table, Lily elbowed me softly and said, "Your ability to speak our tongue has sparked my interest in you. I wonder what your genetic disposition will tell us if we took samples." Her countenance changed to that of inquisitive and she searched me with her eyes.

"Was that a racist joke?" I was not sure whether there was another way to ask the question, and I regretted it immediately.

She threw her head back and laughed loudly. "Pretty good, right?"

We laughed all the way home. It felt like two old friends or a couple sharing an inside joke. As soon as we got to the gate, we turned to look at each other. Neither one of us said anything for a few moments. She finally spoke up, "It feels surreal that our little microcosm has come to an end."

"Yes, I guess that we will have to do it again sometime." I said it as if I was making a statement but I hoped she would take it as a question and answer.

"We can absolutely do this again. Keep me in the loop on what Dillie is doing. Goodnight, Joseph." She rushed toward me and gave me a hug. A moment of bliss fluttered my soul as she breathed on my neck. She released me first and quickly walked through the gate and back towards her room.

I relished in the events of the day as I sauntered towards my abode. I finally reached my room for a good night's sleep.

Chapter 9

The sound of a letter slipping under my door woke me from my rest. I surmised Dillie must have brought it to my quarters as I have never noticed a mailroom. The envelope had the address for the slums and my name written in a neat cursive. It looked as if it did not belong to any person but was carefully composed by a machine. It smelled of sandalwood and had a deep red insignia on the back to close it. I pulled out the letter which was folded in half from portrait. The paper was parchment that seemed more like it was from ancient Egyptian times, rather than something more modern. The ink and stroke patterns led me to believe that a quill pen was used to compose the work. I was in awe of the penmanship and the attentiveness to presentation. Whoever wrote this cared a lot about giving this letter personality. The letter said,

Greetings sir:

I cannot go into detail right now but I need to discuss some matter of great importance regarding the Martian movement. It is imperative that we talk as your safety and that of the Martians is on the line. Please meet me near the pecan tree in the garden outside of the town after sunset. Also, please exercise the utmost discretion on your doings, you can never know who is trustworthy.

Thank you

Anonymous

Suspicious? Yes, this letter was. However, I needed to know. My professors always claimed that I was not thorough enough for doctorate research. They even complained that I did not go far enough or deep enough to gain that added perspective. I am not sure if this was what they meant. Waiting to have a secret meeting in the garden near the slums of the very beings who would change the way humans viewed the universe and humanity made my skin crawl with anticipation. I wondered what this person had to say. I pondered telling Dillie or Lily, but I knew that I could not. The writer asked me to exercise discretion and telling them would certainly cause an incident. I needed to know more or I might have never been able to get real answers if I had either of those two with me.

I waited nervously for any noise in the hallway to die down before I sneaked out of the slums. I asked myself why I was sneaking. What was I worried about? Something about this did not feel right, but I knew that I needed to go. I resolved in my mind to talk to Dillie and Lily as soon as the meeting was over.

As I walked into the garden, the air turned chilled. It felt as if the heat was sucked out by a vacuum and replaced with freezing air. I could see my breath and my body was shivering uncontrollably. I should have brought a jacket, but I did not realize that nights got this cold. A light breeze began and caused the trees to sway. A moment passed, and I heard rustling in the bank of bushes. I thought I saw movement, but I could not be sure. Now, I was beginning to perspire. How was this possible? I was clutching my arms together because it was so cold on my skin, but my body was so hot that I was sweating. I felt scared and overwhelmed.

The branches from the trees looked sinister, as if monsters were rising out of the ground. Their eyes glowed in the light of the moon. My soul shivered in response. I noticed that the garden did not have vegetation anymore. It seemed a little odd in my mind, but I was unable to focus. I heard the faint whispers of souls, crying through the trees while they moved. I had enough. I needed to leave and I thought I was starting to get sick. I was about to turn to leave when I see a figure appear in the dark. It was standing still. Was it watching me this whole time? Was it doing something to my mind? I felt compelled to walk towards it, but my feet remained still. It began running towards me. I thought I was crazy. This was not happening. I walked towards the figure, but it was starting to seem more human now. Then, I saw a man. A tall man who had broad shoulders and was wearing a crisp, fitted suit. His neck was that of a body builder's and his hands look rough from repeated abuse. He was standing almost a foot taller than me at 6'6. He was standing still, and I proceed closer to the mysterious man. The moon reflected off his glasses and there seemed to be a scowl on his face. I looked harder and he managed to contort a smile, but it felt unnatural. His teeth were all canines and his tongue was slightly forked.

The figure then spoke to me, startling me out of my musing. "Good evening Joseph, my name is Fien Dioni. I apologize for all the secrecy, but I have to protect my client's interest."

His voice was not natural. The words came out like a growl yet with the gentleness of a whisper. Everything he said seemed like it was carefully rehearsed and planned. He had a mastery of the English language. I replied, "It's quite all right sir, what can I do for you?"

"Well, my client has noted the struggle of the Martians and is interested in providing assistance. He is also interested in your work." Each word from Fien took a bite into my soul, causing me a great amount of fear.

Uncertain as to how I might respond, I offered, "thank you. I am just an academic who is working to tell the story of the Martians and provide perspective from a non-Martian source."

"Excellent work, sir, I know that your research will prove to be influential." With that statement, he moved forward slightly. It was as if he was floating or skating. I started to feel sick again.

Something about this just was not right. Why would anyone be interested in my work? I was not much of a writer, but I gained an audience with the most influential Martian on this planet, Dillie. His face was conveying mildness, but I could sense that every word was just short of being slithered. Maybe my senses were off, but I knew this was not what it seemed. I needed to find out more.

"Thank you again, but what would you like from me?"

He said, "Yes sir, as I said, my client is interested in the Martians' struggle. He knows how hard it is to persevere in a place where others do not want you to exist. He would like to offer aid in the form of providing food for the Martians."

"That is an excellent way to help." I pondered for a moment. This sounded too good to be true. I appreciated the offer, but I thought about how much it would cost me. How much would it cost the Martians? This could not be an appropriate decision for me to make on their behalf. "But why are you approaching me? Why not go to the leadership directly?"

"You see Joseph, you are the key to all of this. You are the only human who has ever been invited into a Martian compound to document their lives, and you have proven trustworthy to the Martians. We would like to leverage that as part of our public relations campaign." When he finished his pitch, he straightened his posture as if he just completed a sales pitch.

Skeptical, my only reaction came through in my tone, "okay. What would you like for me to do?"

Fien's wicked smile revealed itself again. I sensed the kicker coming. "You see Joseph, in order to equip the Martians with the sustenance they need, they cannot be distracted with delusions of grandeur."

I was shocked, but also a bit insulted by that remark. "What does that mean?" I did not intend for my annoyance to come through, but I suppressed it.

The smug smirk on his face became wider. I remembered thinking how much it must have hurt to hold his face like that. He offered his explanation. "It means that we are asking you to step back from your writings and we will give the Martians all the food they could ever want. They will eat like kings every day and not a single Martian will go hungry. We would also want Dillie to be turned over to us for her treachery in the Martian lottery."

That's the sticking point; I knew there was a catch. "Why are you asking this of me?" I thought about 'Dillie's treachery' for a moment, but I refused to be distracted.

His smile widened more. "Joseph, the answer to that question is not so simple. There are certain benefits to keeping the Martians where they are."

I could feel myself getting angry. I did not know if it was the contorted, almost scowling smile on his face, something that I ate for lunch, or the fact that I remember the garden having leaves in the trees just a few days ago. I needed to focus. Anger was not a productive emotion, and maybe I could educate Fien to the truth. I breathed and responded, "I know what you want and you cannot have it. More than any food that you may offer, the Martians want equality. This is their principal tenant. 'The right to live surpasses everything a Martian shall desire. Martian philosophy and values number one.' They want to be recognized as fellow citizens of this world and be given the opportunity to partake. Not go through some lottery and only accept those who box themselves into a human template. I will no longer talk to you, you need to leave. Now!"

His face contorted to the scowl. I could tell that my response surprised and angered him. He quickly reverted back to the canine smile, and he bowed as he receded into the trees. With his departure, my anger subsided, my spirit calmed, and the garden seemed to regain its tranquility. Who was this Fien? Why was he asking me to destroy the Martians one chance at equality, in exchange for bread?

This was troubling to my mind. Now that I was thinking about it, my body was exhausted. I perspired all over the sheets and I was breathing hard. Why was this encounter so exhausting? I sat up in my bed, asking myself if I had just dreamt that whole experience. It felt so real, but I freed my mind to sleep again.

Chapter 10

I arose from my slumber feeling more worn out than I should have felt following eight hours of sleep. My body ached all over when I tried to move off the bed. I laid on the mattress for a few more minutes. Unable to become comfortable, I powered through my pain and prepared myself to find Dillie.

First, I walked outside to find the garden and tree leaves intact, and a nice warm day outside. I shuddered at my mental state for conjuring such an encounter. But it felt more real than me walking around at that moment.

Walking through the harrowed corridor, I found my way to Dillie's strange office. She was seated in a lotus position on the desk facing the window, away from the door. I thought she might have planned to be seen doing this activity. Maybe Lily's distrust had influenced me.

"Meditating?" I asked to make conversation, but not interested in the answer.

"Not quite, I am pondering." She rose in a swift motion and flipped off the desk onto the floor. She held both hands in the air as if she had finished a routine in a gymnastics competition. I was impressed, but tried to temper my enthusiasm. She asked, "Are you planning to update me on your findings? Or is this visit a personal one?"

I decided to try and get an answer about her business with me. "Dillie, why did you choose me for this work? So many other humans to choose from and here I am. Why?" I felt like this would be the only way to get a straight answer from her.

"What makes you think it was deliberate?" Her question back to me was quick and seemed planned. She looked at me for a few moments, waiting on my response. "Is this because of your secret dinner with Lily?"

I stopped breathing. How did she know? I felt at a disadvantage because of the question I was not prepared to answer. I did not have the upper hand in this conversation. "We did not...I mean, we were discussing..."

Dillie raised her hand to quiet me. "It is better if you do not lie to me, so do not tell me what happened. Whatever you two are up to, be careful. Humans and Martians have very little in common. It is obvious that you like her, but Lily's priority defers to the betterment of the Martian cause." She crossed the room and walked to her leather chair to sit. She picked up a pen and began to write.

I had to take a real chance and surprise her. I knew it was only a dream, but maybe there was some truth to it. "What about your treachery in the Martian lottery? Can we talk about that?" I could tell that question surprised her.

She stared at the desk for a moment, pen slipped from her fingers. "Why would you..." and then she caught herself, "Are you joking? You know nothing about what you are speaking. I have given everything so Martians can have a piece of the privilege that humans are born with." She dismissed the conversation by going back to her work.

I realized Dillie was at a loss for words. She always had something to say. I shuddered at the thought that I may have experienced in real life whatever I dreaded, but this was a great feeling to have the advantage over her. "I am not joking, I have strong reason to believe that you are involved in something that you do not want to be known publicly. You do not have to tell me, but I caution you to tread carefully." I am not sure why I was honest with her, but I was amazed at the truthfulness of my dream.

"Very well Joseph. Truth has a way of coming out of the most unexpected places." Dillie crooked a smile and went back to her work.

I felt a strong urge to pull the string further, but I knew she was done. Dillie was going to regroup and challenge me later.

I ran back through the halls towards Lily's room. The halls were a maze, but I had a general idea of where she might be located. We ended up bumping into each other near the cafe. I told her everything about my dream and the conversation with Dillie.

She grabbed me by the shoulders and dragged me to her office. After closing the door, Lily clapped her hands together and said "I knew it. So, it is the lottery system! We need to figure out what she is doing." She paced the room, a quiet reflection of ideas replaced the excitement of confirmed suspicions.

"Could it be money? Would she take the money and use it for herself?" I asked the most logical question because that was what a human would do.

Lily stopped in place and looked at me while shaking her head. She then studied me for a moment and said "No, unlikely. Dillie is being sneaky, but she has no need for wealth. Martians learned from our troubles on Mars and Earth to not store up treasures which will be claimed by another in due time."

Another tenant; I was impressed with her convictions to follow their law. However, I thought Lily being convinced of Dillie's intentions was presumptuous. "Well, is it possible that there is a prize? I sense that she is making a deal and is overwhelmed with the trade she is making."

Lily remained silent for a moment longer. She walked up to me and examined my face. I felt like Lily was studying me like a scientist does when looking at a creature. "Why did you say that?"

I was confused. "Uh, I considered what I know about her and tried to discern the rest."

"Interesting," Lily said. She ran over to her bookshelf and grabbed a book that looked thousands of years old. "Martian language and ancient text. There is a word for this. Ah, 'mallaime.'"

"What? Malam?" I wondered where this conversation was going.

A look of a good impression crossed her face. Lily said, "yeah, you pronounced it right. It is a term for the type of person that says things like what you just said about Dillie."

I felt like I had messed up with Lily again. Would she be upset at me for making an assumption? Being judgmental was taboo for any culture. She must think I am a terrible person. "I am sorry, I should not have said..."

"Oh no, no, no, Joseph." Lily raised her fingers to my lips to stop me from taking. "It is not bad, it is a good thing. It means you are good a reading others in an accurate manner with extrasensory-like perception."

I felt better and honored that Lily offered me a compliment. She was opening up to me in ways I had never appreciated from anyone else. "Oh good."

She stopped smiling and looked at the floor. "Well, maybe not, this term is specific to Martians. It roughly translates to mean a being who can see truth where it is not always apparent.

Unlike intuition, clairvoyance, or discernment, this gift is capable of seeing into another being's heart."

"How would that apply to me? I am not doing that." I leaned against the wall and stared at Lily. I wondered where she was going, still flattered that I was on her mind.

"Well, I need to examine you more, but I have a hypothesis based on your gift of the Martian tongue. It makes me think you may have other similarities to Martians, including temperamental and biological similarities."

What was she saying? I am human, I look like a human, I have the biology of a human, but how could I explain what I was experiencing? Knowing Martian, a language which no human can speak or hear?

"A blood test!" Lily ran over to me and shook me. "I could have your blood tested to explain how you are able to hear and speak Martian. It may also give us an indication as to how you developed this ability and what else could happen to you."

I shuddered at the thought of a needle and the possibilities of what it may find. Considering the stories that have been told over the years, I wondered what the other humans who claim to have been abducted would say to my willful consent. "Okay," was my response.

She grabbed my hand and we tarried down the corridor to the rendezvous room where we would conduct her experiment. The other Martians did not notice, or maybe not care about us walking the hallway holding hands. But I felt a spark. We walked into a closet that had two chairs facing each other and an array of medical equipment. She grabbed some nitrile gloves, three blood packs, a tourniquet, an alcohol prep pad, and a bandaid. She laid them neatly on the table next to my chair.

I glanced at the equipment and said, "It seems like you are planning on taking a lot of blood from me."

"Well, we Martians must probe human companions to determine suitability for consumption." She stared at me and started creeping slowly towards me in a trance. Her mouth was open and drool was dribbling down her lips.

My jaw dropped in shock and fear. I placed my hands up and backed away saying her name as I tried to ascertain a path to my freedom.

And then she stopped, falling to the floor laughing. "Are you serious? You were so scared. Of course I am not going to eat you. I will get the plasma preparation tubes." She stood up and walked out and into another room.

I sat and thought about how much she had opened up to me. I felt a strong attraction to her for the brilliance of her mind and how I felt in sync with her soul. It felt like we moved at the same speed, and I enjoyed the exercise she gave my mind when we talked. I relished in the possibilities of a love that could be until the door opened.

Lily came in and administered the blood test as carefully as a first-time nurse. She said, "I want this to remain quiet and I only trust myself to do this."

I wondered how she could believe that she was the only trustworthy one since Martians were not 'fallen' creatures. The whole experience lasted three minutes and was virtually painless. She promised to alert me to the results and then we exited the closet to find Dillie standing there.

Chapter 11

Dillie stood at the entrance to the closet. I stood there frozen, as if I was caught in the act of doing something illegal. I gave myself away by raising my hands in surrender.

"What are you doing?" I felt Dillie asking the question to me although her eyes remained fixated on Lily.

"I was showing Joseph around and wanted him to see our nursing area. It occurred to me that he was not familiar with Martian biology, so I was showing him the equipment." I was shocked at the ease with which Lily offered a fictitious explanation for our doings. I lowered my hands as she looked over to me while saying, "As you can clearly see from the bandage on his arm, I decided to provide a demonstration by drawing a small vial of blood."

"I bet you enjoyed the speed and painless extraction process we have in drawing blood. Technology humanity has yet to discover." Dillie engaged us in this conversation, but did not seem to buy the story. I was working through a list of jokes to interject and lighten the mood when Dillie asked, "What about your blood, Lily? Should you offer Joseph a chance to see your blood? Never mind, I came here because I needed to ask you both a question. Have either of you been leaking information internal to the Martian community to the humans?"

We both shook our heads. I thought to myself who would do something like that and then remembered the dream I had with Fien.

Dillie lingered a look at both of us for a few moments apiece while she thought. "Okay, but I am concerned about how close you two are becoming. The private conversations and the late-night trysts are suspicious. And I am not the only one who notices. I think your allegiance is to one another as opposed to the greater Martian good. Lily, I am going to recommend to the board that you be removed from influence until we can evaluate your interests in Joseph and whether he is influencing your agenda."

Lily's face contorted so much so that she looked like she might explode. The hair on my skin crawled with anticipation for what might come next. However, no words came from Lily. She exhaled strongly and said, "Maybe Joseph is influencing my agenda and viewpoints. But I did not bring him here. Dillie, why did you bring him here? Why are you still leading the Martians? Our tradition demanded you step down years ago. I am the only being who is concerned for the well-being of the Martians. You, on the other hand, seem to only care about staying in power. Since you are the absolute authority for us, if anyone is leaking information to humans, I would say that you should already know. I bet you are the person leaking information and using my private interactions, on my own time with another being, as a basis to ruin me. Tell the truth, Dillie." Lily stood strong and glared at Dillie.

I felt proud of Lily in that moment for standing up to Dillie. The older Martian did not flinch, but smirked. I wanted to put Dillie in her place, but I did not have anything to say. I knew Lily's allegations would be unfounded and would not stop Dillie from crushing Lily if it came to their individual words. Then, I remembered my dream. I knew it was a long shot, but if there was any truth to his story, I could scare Dillie. Before she could react to Lily, I said, "Who is Fien Dioni, Dillie?"

I think that got to Dillie, because her eyes opened in horror at the realization that I knew. Lily did not notice Dillie's reaction because she was looking at me, confused. Dillie exploded in a fit of rage at Lily, ignoring my comment. Dillie yelled at Lily over the accusations and the impartiality of being a leader for Martians. Based on Lily's surprise at Dillie's outburst, I could tell that Lily had not planned for a full-on assault. Lily received Dillie's assault and accepted every word with strong defiance. She kept her facial expression neutral and allowed Dillie to vent in her face until the old Martian ran out of breath. I felt agitated and hurt for Lily, but she did not show any emotional wounds. Dillie huffed and puffed for a few moments and said, "I am sorry Lily. That was unacceptable for me to yell at you and accuse you. My grudge is professional and I know you are not doing anything against your fellow beings."

Lily held up her hands to Dillie's shoulders and accepted the apology. "You know all is forgiven." I noticed that Dillie glanced my way, but she was not going to mention Fien. She knew who he was and that meant that my dream was real and she was tied up with him somehow. My heart hurt for the possibility that Dillie's crime could be revealed. I needed to talk with Lily and struggled to think of an appropriate time.

Lily interrupted my thoughts. "We must evoke the Martian practice of restoration to give us peace. How about we perform the 'kaisoishai' and reflect?"

Kaisoishai. My mind could not place the word, but I assumed it had something to do with a rite of passage. I wondered what Lily was planning to do with Dillie, but it seemed like a private time. I started to leave, but Lily waved me over to them. "Joseph, you should stay with us and reflect as well, since you are a witness."

Dillie smiled, but it was clear from her expression that she was uncomfortable with doing whatever Lily was describing. "He would not understand, he is human. Besides, other Martians may not appreciate his being here. They would resist something like this happening."

Lily touched Dillie's shoulder. "You are the last one of the three. I am sure Martians would accept your wisdom, and not one of us ever challenges you except me. If the other Martians were to have witnessed our argument in front of this human, they would agree that we must go through with the prayer in his presence."

Lily then touched my shoulder, "Joseph, we are about to perform an ancient Martian ritual that allows us to reflect and forgive one another. Everyone who was involved, even the witnesses, lays hands on one another and offers forgiveness and presents one mind. It has a soul cleansing effect on the parties involved. I'm not sure you will feel anything as a human, but at least you will have the opportunity to experience a tradition that is not very common among Martians."

Dillie looked at me, mentally suggesting that I bow out. I looked back at her, confused. Dillie said, "I do not think that Joseph should participate."

"Why, Dillie? Since he is human, nothing can happen to him. Even though he would not understand, it would still be okay since he was here. Joseph, just think about how all of this made you feel and reflect on your position in life to improve the world. That is it," Lily insisted and looked at Dillie, then she bowed her head, ready for prayer.

Dillie released an exasperated sigh in fear, placed her hands on Lily's and my shoulders, and lowered her head. Something did not feel right about this prayer and my mind kept replaying Lily's comment about nothing happening to me.

The prayer was unintelligible. The groans emanating from Dillie were strong and heartfelt. I sensed pain and healing from Lily's groans. I could feel the sensations with my bones and my soul stirred at her entreat. I felt a burning sensation as I struggled to stay latched on to them. Some of their words started to become intelligible, much like a person who was familiar with a few words in a language. The prayer ended and I let go of their shoulders. Both Dillie and Lily looked at me with concern.

"Are you okay?" Dillie asked while grabbing my arm. I wanted to stumble and fall, but I fought to retain my composure. My soul felt heavy with the flooding of information into my body. I felt detached from my body and slinked away from Dillie with everything I could muster to look okay.

"I am fine, thank you. But I should depart and write out my observations. Lily, would you please escort me back to my quarters so I can ask you some questions?" She nodded and ran to my side and grabbed my arm. We turned a corner and looked behind us to make sure Dillie was nowhere to be found. I grabbed the handle of a door to a conference room and we went inside. "What did you do to me?" I whispered once the door closed with my face hitting the ground as I collapsed.

Lily ran towards me, lifted me into a chair, and expressed a mixture of regret and excitement, "I am sorry Joseph. I did not mean to hurt you. I had an inclination, but I did not know for sure about the effect it would have on you. You are an amazing being to experience that and be able to walk your way here. There are so many questions I have for you."

The flurry of questions from Lily clouded my mind with answers that I could not have known. She asked me about historical events on Earth and general questions about the extent of the universe today. She asked me about my parents and about my biological characteristics that would allow me to be human, but also capable to Martian power. It was like my eyes were opened and I had a complete knowledge of the universe around me. It was jumbled, but beginning to formulate a complete picture.

Lily said, "Explain to me the extent of your knowledge."

The answer presented itself to me like a meal on a silver platter. It did not emanate from my mind, but the statement was original and my own. "It is like I know who God is. Not in abstract, I can comprehend His enormity." My eyes were fixated on Lily, who was in shock.

"I cannot believe it." Lily sat in a chair for a moment and leaned back, staring at the ceiling.

I became a bit concerned. "Lily, what is going on? Please help me understand," I pleaded with her, hoping she would awake from her shock. I thought of all the consequences and I felt fainter. I leaned my head back some more, prepared to die.

Lily ran over to me and slapped me awake. She explained that my mind was opening up to the reality of the universe. My mind was unlocking multiple millennia of Martian knowledge. The ritual of restoration has the effect of passing on the Martian gifts available to all unfallen beings. Any time the

Martian authority laid it hands on other beings in prayer, whether that be 'kaisoishai' or any of their other rituals, it conferred the ability to understand the language and bestowed the collective knowledge of the ancients as well as the greater purpose behind the Universe. Humans, being fallen in their nature, were thought to be unable to receive this gift. Lily considered it a mystery and promised to do more research on my blood to understand what was happening.

As the fog in my mind began to clear, I could understand what she meant. My frail emotional state threatened to lash out on multiple occasions due to the amount of new information I was presented with, but I tempered myself. The knowledge of the universe kept unpacking on me and the grandness of it all cause great marveling within me. I was most impressed with the unpacking of the Martian language, sensing the part of my body that created the groans and the exact manner with which I say certain phrases. Also, the writing and the rich tradition of the beings that traverse from the fourth planet. Other beings and their languages. Speaking of the name of the planet—Mars was not her name, but 'Dworea.' The meaning of the word was 'gift.' Such beauty and grace. The knowledge was continually flowing in and I could not handle any more right now.

I rose from my chair, I limped to the door, thanking Lily on the way out. As I reached for the door, Lily asked, "Who is Fien?"

I sighed, tired from the events of the day. "The missing link for Dillie's private exploits." I grabbed the handle and slugged back to my room without another word. I sat on the bed, trying to quiet my mind enough to allow me to rest. My body transitioned to slumber as quickly as I could lay my head on the pillow.

Chapter 12

I dreamed that Lily was gently caressing my shoulder. My body resisted the urge to embrace her. I was not quite sure how, but I thought I had fallen in love. Looking into her eyes, I felt an insatiable desire to kiss her. Just one simple kiss. She looked at me longingly. I could feel the warmth from her hand. She loved me, and I her. I was tired, and this dream was not real.

As I fell back into the groggy dream world of her love, I awoke suddenly to a more violent rousing. This was not a dream and Lily was trying to wake me. "Please Joseph, get up. We must go now, we don't have much time."

Lily was wearing another pink silky robe that had stars over her breast. Everything was perfect on her body. The length of the dress came to the middle of her thigh to reveal two strong and smooth green legs. The neckline of her gown showed the center of her chest. The sleeves were the perfect length, stopping right below her elbows, to show the perfect texture of her forearms. I pulled her closer to me. The fire that burned inside craved to know her. I resisted lingering on any thoughts that may have lasted longer than that.

I wondered what was so urgent. "Where are we going Lily? I am very tired."

Her big brown eyes focused on mine. Lily leaned in close to me, or maybe I pulled her close. Whichever it was, she was so close that the whiskers on my cheek rose to graze the side of her face. Her breathing was steady, and my heart slowed to match its pace. Each breath tickled my soul. Her flowing hair draped across my lips like a blanket of silk. Her hands tightly gripped my shoulders which mimicked love's warm embrace. She turned her head slowly until her lips were almost touching my ears.

"Please Joseph, I need you to just trust me by doing what I am asking of you. The truth will reveal itself in due time."

With that statement, she rose away from me, just far enough for us to make eye contact. We sat there for a moment and stared at one another. My hands were holding her waist and I made my move towards her. She moved towards me. Lily softly kissed me on the lips. The kiss lingered in a peck as we sat frozen. Nothing more to the kiss than that. After about ten seconds, we gently tore ourselves away from one another as Lily stood from the bed and turned her back.

I levitated off the bed and on to my feet. I was stunned to say the least. I walked up behind her and lightly touched her shoulder. I said, "Lily," softly and turned her around. She was tearing a little in her eyes and looked at me. My eyes began to well up with tears. Knowing the joy of love for another at this level roused a new sense of purpose in me.

Before I could make another move, she grabbed my shoulder and pushed me away. Lily said, "Dillie knows my heart better than I know it myself. Unfortunately, she did not account for the fact that I would not let it distract me from my purpose. We must go now." With that, we exited the room in night clothes as I followed Lily down the dark corridor.

The colorful walls were no match for the gloom of nighttime in this building. The halls felt more like a labyrinth in a Victorian era castle with the cinder blocks stacked on top of one another and the colors not visible. Dimly lit hallways and color absence gave off an ominous feel as we continued on our journey. We were walking faster now. I tried to focus

on walking since I was so tired. I could sense the urgency in
Lily's stride. She seemed conflicted and yet determined.
Whatever we were about to see, she was solely focused on
getting there. I tried to talk with her, but she quickly hushed
me.

"Quiet Joseph," Lily hissed in a hushed tone. "We are
doing something that will add a new level of complexity to the
Martian movement. We need to be ready."

At that moment, we stopped. We were at the entrance to
Dillie's quarters. The lights were off and the door was open.
We tiptoed through the threshold into a small office set up
with a desk, red leather chair, a file drawer, and a rather large
wooden coat closet.

"Joseph, look through the desk," Lily barked.

"What are we looking for," I countered, starting to feel
uncomfortable with all the secrecy.

Lily looked to me again with annoyance. "I am not
completely sure, but there must be a piece of paper or
anything that we can find to use against her."

It was my turn to be upset. "Lily, you have been a fairly
rational and reasonable person up to this point. You are rifling
through your colleagues' personal effects. How is this
appropriate? How would you feel if Dillie did this to you? And
now you are asking me to participate in this treasonous activity
with little to no discussion as to why? This is not okay. Even if
Dillie is in the wrong, you are violating someone's privacy. Tell
me now what is happening, or you can do this by yourself."

Lily looked at me stunned. I could tell that she did not
expect me to lash out at her in this manner, but I was on the
brink of becoming furious. She looked down at the floor for a
few moments and muttered to herself. After several moments,

she lifted her head and met my eyes. "I do not know what Dillie is doing, but I know that we are receiving considerable sums of money that is not traceable. This money is coming from somewhere and everyone is just so trusting of Dillie. I need to know what she is up to in her efforts to get these funds. Whatever it is cannot be legal or ethical."

At that moment, I realized why Lily was such a problem for Dillie. She was the ultimate adversary to progress. Some people believe that the greater good was achieved through the murky waters of compromise. An extreme example would be a local drug dealer who paid the college tuition for all the local kids. To the ones who are burdened to uphold the law, the drug dealer was a criminal, to the beneficiaries of one's generosity, the drug dealer was a hero. It all really depends. Lily was a big problem to Dillie as her ethics would not allow her to stoop to such a level to provide for those needy Martians.

I carefully considered what to say next. Dillie was up to something, and I could sense that without my expanded knowledge. In addition to that, Fien telling me about her confirmed there may be reason to do as Lily asked. "If your intuition is correct, then we need to follow up on your suspicion. I will look in the desk."

Lily smiled and mouthed, "Thank you."

I looked at the desk and proceeded to go through it. The desk was made of Chester wood. It looked like it weighed 500 pounds. Looking closely at the wood, I could tell that the surface was carefully etched to create a tapestry of what I could safely assume were Martian symbols. My mind wanted to say more, but I did not have time. This desk was a work of art more than it was a place to do work. The one drawer on the desk had a handle that looked like it had dragon scales. This was a custom-made desk for a person with expensive taste. I tried the handle to only be rejected by a lock.

I turned from the desk to gaze upon Lily opening the wooden coat closet. The doors looked like the entrance to a castle. They opened with the characteristic sound of a heavy door and sat in place about halfway open. I silently tread to the entrance and closed it slightly to look behind it.

Just then, I saw a faint glow of light down the hall. Someone was coming this way. I turned and bumped into Lily. Before she could protest my clumsiness, I placed my right hand over her mouth and my left hand up to my lips to shush her. She nodded obediently.

"We have to hide," I said. We looked around for a moment. We could hear the footsteps coming closer, Dillie's shrill voice coming through as a hum.

Lily began to panic. "We can't let her find us in here."

I grabbed her by the shoulders and shoved her into the coat closet. I then proceeded to jump in after her. However, the door did not fully close. I whispered, "Lily, can you back up just an inch more?"

I could hear her lightly shuffling as I was struggling to pull the door closed completely. Fortunately, it was heavy enough to keep me firmly in place.

"I cannot move anymore," Lily whispered.

I accepted her reasoning and settled with a slight crack in the door. Hopefully Dillie would not look too closely and notice that someone was in her closet.

We settle into the closet and held a long breath of silence until the door creaked and the familiar footsteps of Ms. Dillie Johnson egressed into the room.

The steps stopped in what I believe was the middle of the room. "Mm, I don't remember leaving the door closed," Dillie's voice mused loudly. She was acting strangely for someone who considered herself to be alone right now.

Just then, the footsteps were clopping towards the closet until they stopped right in front. I saw the left side of this frail Martian being. I could smell the fragrance of lilacs and cherries. Her peach colored t-shirt was draped over her frail and bony frame like an ill-fitting dress that was meant for a fuller figured person. Her pants were some yellow capri pants with no shoes or socks.

Dillie stood at the door for a moment too long. I was preparing myself for what I needed to say or do to disorient her so we could escape. Lily started pinching my right arm. Her nails were digging deep into the top dermal layers of my skin. Her breathing was almost hyperventilating and her heart had the beat of a marching band. We were caught.

Then Dillie turned away from the door. "I guess I could just give him a call," Dillie quipped.

The words alone almost spooked us out of the closet. Lily started breathing again and I relaxed. While we considered the rare fortune of not being discovered, Dillie walked into full view and sat at the desk.

Through the crease in the door, I looked at Dillie sitting at the desk as she stared at the phone. She sighed and proceeded to look through a Rolodex. It was at that very moment when I realized just how worn Dillie looked. Her eyelids seemed heavy, like someone who had not slept in years. I wondered if she suffered insomnia. Her skin was pale and lines had begun to form all over her face. Her hands trembled as she fumbled with the items on her desk.

She stopped at a name on her Rolodex. Then she grabbed the phone and began to dial.

As she was dialing the number, she stopped and looked up directly at me. My heart stopped; did she know I was there? There was no possible way for her to see me. She just stared at the blank space that was supposed to be the closet for a moment. She whipped a massive smirk across her face and planted her finger over her lips. To my surprise, she knew I was there.

A deep and shrill voice answered on the other line, "Dillie, we have been waiting." The voice sounded like a local politician.

Dillie looked down, and began talking, "good evening Mr. Dixon. I apologize for calling you so late in the evening, I needed to make sure that the conditions were appropriate for the conversation."

There were a few grunts on the other end of the line, but everyone remained silent.

She glanced my way one more time and then begins again. "Per our previous conversations, I believe that I have the right product to meet the needs of the humans' technological developments..."

Just then, a fear started to overcome my senses. It was a wariness like an ominous presence was nearby. Mr. Dixon immediately interrupted Dillie, "I know that you are piecemealing the information to us. The technology to rebuild the Martian spacecraft has always been in your mind. You sold us portions of the technology over the years. Did you expect that this would remain secret? I know you know the full secret of the Martian technology. One of your own finally sold you out. It took some time, but he started talking. We have paid you billions to research what you already knew. You shorted us on the space shuttle program, Dillie. We want everything or we are going to crush your movement. This is no idle threat, ma'am, and I will not put up with this anymore."

Lily and I were stunned. The air escaped from the closet, and we tensed up.

Dillie looked again at the closet with a relief that could only be attributed to a horrible truth that had been revealed. She placed her finger over her mouth again and regained her composure with a few breaths. She leaned into the phone and said, "I understand that you feel a certain way about my products. I can assure you that I have dealt with you fairly. Regardless, I am the only being who had the knowledge to provide you with the technology to achieve your purposes. Do as you must, but you will only sabotage yourselves in the long run. Thank you and goodbye."

With that statement, Dillie hung up the phone. She sighed and placed her hands over her face. Following her quiet reflection, Dillie then turned and met my eyes on the closet. She smiled, got up, and left, closing the door.

Lily erupted us from the closet knocking me onto my face.

"I cannot believe that she did this. Why would she do it? Only a select few Martians are chosen to hold the secrets of the technology. When we were captured at Area 51, all the Martians remained resolved to not divulge who held those secrets no matter what. Dillie is the last one remaining. We were hoping to have a new class soon, but Dillie said that she should hold on to the secrets as they had no way to secure the resources without human intervention, the same humans who imprisoned us. So, she decided to hold the secret alone to protect the information from humans who would seek to exploit this for unfruitful purposes. I cannot believe that she solely held onto this information to sell it for her purposes. Joseph, she must be stopped. We must confront her."

Lily's indignation against Dillie reached a level of intensity I had never seen out of her before. My senses burned hot and told me of the rage that Lily was feeling.

I knew this was as bad as it probably seemed. I stood in place staring blankly into the wall for a moment to process what had happened. My next step was important to how things could have turned out. My mind started reviewing what I observed: Dillie knew we were in the closet, hence her motioning for us to remain quiet. I was the only one who saw that gesture. Whatever she was doing, she wanted us to hear, due to the phone being on speaker. Things did not add up as to why Dillie was doing what she did. I needed to find out what was going on. If I confronted Dillie myself, I was running the risk of losing Lily's trust, and any hope for affection. However, this may have been my only chance to get the truth. One thing was for sure, Lily was too emotional to question Dillie.

I carefully crafted my words. "Lily, it is best that we get you to bed, leave your questions for Dillie until tomorrow." I held my breath and let the silence linger for a moment too long. I could feel myself gulp for air and sweat run down the left side of my face. It was difficult to lie to her.

She looked at me with her fists clenched into tight balls. She let out a sigh and nodded her head in agreement. "You are right, I am tired anyway. Dillie is not going to run from the compound tonight."

I walked Lily back to her quarters and proceeded to mine. I needed to think, but I was exhausted. I promised myself that

I would wake up in an hour, well before dawn, to question Dillie.

Chapter 13

My hour-long nap had proven to not be useful, as my body struggled to move following the alarm. I kept reminding myself why I was doing this, but my exhaustion was reaching new heights due to my lack of sleep and the mental awareness that continually unpacked the knowledge of the universe on me. I made it over to the vanity, took a shot of ice cold water to my face, and slapped myself one time. Then, I felt I was ready.

I snuck out into the hallway. I walked down the old corridor and to the room where I saw Dillie for the first time.

She was seated in front on her easel and painting on the canvas. Her old voice croaked "Is she sleep?"

"She was an emotional wreck. Why did you not confront us when you realized that we were hiding in the closet? Why can you not see that this level of manipulation is no way to pass the torch? She has been through enough..."

Just then, Dillie interrupted me and said, "I do not need you to explain how a Martian handles Martian business. For your information, I made a calculated decision. If Lily had been the one to see me, then the call would have never happened as she would have burst out of the closet as soon as I lifted my finger to my mouth. She does not have much humor, and that gesture would have stopped this little revelation. You see Joseph, it had to be you. Lily is too emotionally invested to have gotten to this point."

Dillie then lifted herself and gravitated towards me. Her face betrayed her weariness. I kept my emotions and comments to myself. Dillie wanted to talk, I intended for her to talk.

Dillie sighed. "Very well. I know when it is my turn to reveal my cards, so here you go. Back when the Martian technical minds were discussing a path to equality, we were a disorganized group with a lot of poor and hungry beings to make decisions for. We were the technical elite on the ship that was captured and eventually brought to Area 51. The three of us were not trying to make decisions, but the lack of true leadership and a democratic process prevented us from delegating what we were doing. So, we decided to release secrets of Martian technology in pieces that were of no particular use without the proper materials and calculations. Being very advanced, we were able to out think humans and write equations that limited human innovation and forced their dependence on us at irregular intervals. It worked perfectly, but humans proved to be much smarter, greedier, and more resourceful than we estimated."

Dillie smiled again. Despite her countenance, I could sense her anger with humanity. She continued on with her story. "Humans are efficient monsters of industry, but their inter-competition keeps them from true progress. They also have a nasty habit of excluding large portions of their own, who have great potential for technological creation, in favor of a privileged few. Beyond all of that, humans eventually started to figure us out. We had to write more detailed calculations, giving them more accurate information. This proved disastrous, as the human mind is far more capable than previously imagined and they were able to recreate the technology in some instances..."

Dillie stopped talking and looked at me. I had never seen a Martian's lips quiver before, but her facial expression and the surprised look on her face was the most human that I had ever seen her. So many questions and so little time to hear the story. I suppressed my desire to probe and silently urged her to continue.

Dillie then said, "I am not sure about the other two, as we have been out of contact for years, but I have witnessed pieces of human ingenuity with Martian engineering and it is staggeringly beautiful. They were partially unsuccessful in recreating our flying saucers, but they managed to build unmanned and manned rockets from nothing over the course of eighty years. I believe they are now very close to the flying saucer technology and that may be due to my underestimation of them. I believe this is so because of their response in the latest phone calls. Joseph, they know that I have been withholding key information. They will certainly come for me in one way or another. If they do not, word will get out and the Martians will prosecute me under Martian law. Whatever it is, I accept my fate. It is the funding source for the Martians that I am concerned about. We had trouble maintaining with so little, and it will be impossible to meet needs when we are exposed."

I stared at Dillie. I felt the pain in her soul. I sensed the amount of sorrow, not for herself, but for those Martians who never had a say in this whole matter. All of her work would be dissected and misconstrued to be that of a greedy being who was committing crimes against her fellow beings for financial gain, just like the bad humans. Nothing but a juicy story to further the discrimination of Martians.

I could not let that happen. I said, "No Dillie, let me talk to Lily. She will be more reasonable if she hears it from me. I can help her understand the magnitude of the situation."

Just then, a voice rose out of the shadows, "I understand just fine from this vantage." It was Lily. She walked into the light. She was wearing her pink nightgown with bunny slippers. It was impossible to take her seriously except for the blank expression on her face. She did not seem sad, but she was not very happy. She waded to the table and sat across from Dillie. She did not look at me once.

I began to explain before she blurted out, "Shut up Joseph. I am well aware of what you think and I am also aware of the magnitude of this situation." I shut my mouth and stared at Lily. I could tell that Dillie was looking at me with probably as surprised an expression as she would ever have.

"Dillie, look at me please. This is a Martian matter and does not concern humans."

It was Dillie's turn to be irritated as she said, "Now that is unfair, Lily. You can be upset, but you know he belongs here just as much as you do."

Lily's face turned a darker shade of green as she prepared to respond to the comment. But then she stopped. She took three breaths and sat back in her chair. She maintained her gaze upon Dillie and calmly said, "You are correct. I am being unfair to Joseph in a sense. My anger is of a more personal type and I must detach myself from that for the moment as we process what happens next. As he has proven himself a valuable ally and a skilled mediator, his gift will prove useful for the plethora of issues that will arise in this discussion."

Lily then turned to me with the same blank expression. Her hands neatly intertwined with one another as she said, "Furthermore, he is already involved in this mess and I would rather not bring any others so that the story would leak before we have had time to control the flow of information."

Dillie sat there quietly for a moment looking at both of us. She would look for a moment or two and then switch back to the other person. Dillie was calculating who she could appeal to in this circumstance. I am certain that she was finally aware of how bad things were about to get for her. I did not know Martian law to the fullest extent, but my mind would begin to unpack the deep truths and context for Dworean law. The gravity of Dillie's offense first dawned on me and then the law itself.

Lily started speaking first. "Dillie, I think you know that your actions are unacceptable. I also understand what you did and why you did it. My question for you is: what do you propose we do about this?"

Dillie sat for a moment. She stared down at the table and began to draw circles. She drew very large circles slowly. The circles kept getting smaller and smaller inside of the larger circles until she just dotted the center. She looked up at Lily and smiled. "Kill me."

My jaw dropped. My knowledge confirmed this offense was punishable by death, but I never expected Dillie to be so resolved about it.

Lily turned to me, "Joseph, as you know, Martian society is a hierarchal structure. These are very defined and may call for capital punishment in certain cases. However, Dillie knows just as well as anyone else that the wellbeing of the Martian population as a whole could not survive such a blow, especially the scandal and speculation that would result from her public death. Furthermore, we have not done such a thing since landing on Earth, as it would not be well understood with humans. Dillie is just trying to shock you. She knows how overloaded your mind must be right now. Her punishment needs to be administered and severe, but I request you suggest discretion."

Lily turned her gaze back to Dillie. Dillie was no longer smiling. I sat for a moment and pondered how to move past this situation. Lily was correct; even if Dworean law called for Dillie to die, killing her would bring about questions they would not want to answer. Besides, being the only remaining Dworean technology keeper made her too valuable to die.

Lily started talking again to break my musings. "Dillie has committed treason against the Dworean beings. The technology that she had provided the humans places them in danger, as there are strongholds in the universe that will invade should they discover that humanity has advanced capabilities. Dillie does not know the extent of the humans' knowledge nor does she know who informed the humans of her treachery. Considering that I am not partial in this situation, I cannot make a judgment."

Lily again turns to me. Her look was as vacant as two strangers interacting on business. "Joseph, since you have knowledge of what Dillie has done and you are interested in preserving the greater Martian good, how about you provide a judgment and a sentence? Take your time and think carefully, what you decide will be legally binding, even if the agreement is made in secret. All it takes is a couple of witnesses. We will retire and let you think overnight. Is tomorrow afternoon okay for us to convene and deliver judgement? You are free to decline, but we would rather not involve the board in something this delicate."

It was Dillie's turn to be surprised. Her eyes went wide with her lips not giving away surprise. She looked at me longingly and nodded her head in approval. Lily's gaze remained fixed on me and ignoring Dillie.

"Okay," I said. "I will do my best."

With that, Lily immediately stood from the table and dismissed herself for the night.

Dillie looked at me with a questioning face. "What are you thinking, Joseph? Will you punish me? Your girlfriend will forgive you eventually no matter how this turns out."

I did not need to listen to this right now. I stood and walked out without a word.

I heard Dillie shout from behind me, "See you tomorrow. Love you buddy."

I made my way back to my room and laid on the bed. I was mentally and emotionally exhausted.

I needed to consider what my decision would be before noon tomorrow. So much had happened, and I did not feel prepared to decide one way or the other. A lot of things have happened that made me wonder how we got to this point. Dillie was a master of manipulation and aggravation. She had been making moves since the beginning and most of it to upset Lily. She wanted Lily and me to hear all of that stuff about her selling secrets. Dillie was always making moves and counter moves. Everything she did was to try to reach an end goal. What was her goal? She provoked because she wanted information and asked questions to sway opinions. Deciding in Dillie's favor may not necessarily be what she wanted. However, deciding in Lily's favor may alienate her for good. I needed to make a good decision, because Lily and Dillie were counting on me. Whatever I decided would determine who led the organization, and letting either one of them sway that would be disastrous.

I presented the questions to my consciousness and the evidence began flooding in. My spirit advised me to rest while the information to filled my mind.

'You will have the complete picture tomorrow.' It came from my mouth, but it was my gained understanding speaking. I drifted into slumber on that thought, anticipating tomorrow's decision.

Chapter 14

I awoke late the next morning to Dillie sitting outside of my door. She had a very serious look on her face.

"Joseph, follow me." Dillie waved her hand and motioned for me to follow her. I was tired of Dillie being dramatic about what I was doing, but I followed along without protest. Before I knew it, we were walking down an unfamiliar hall.

This hall had markings of a language completely foreign to me. Their writing looked like pieces of geometry that were intertwined till they formed words. The geometric shapes were stylized and neatly written. I entreated my consciousness to translate, but it struggled to break down the history of the written language.

There were pictures mixed in with the writing in certain places, almost like a story was being told. The landscapes looked like the Amazonian jungle, but with Martian shadows. There were waterfalls and creatures intertwined. The only difference was the color. The sky was a beautiful shade of red. Then there was also pictures of an explosion. I could sense the beauty and the anger that went into the passionate work. I could feel my soul begin to lift. The work was resonating with the very fibers of my existence. I knew that I was meant to be here.

We walked through the big wooden doors with a perfect square on each. The squares had the representation for a right angle, a line going from one corner to another, and words on top that seemed to denote fairness, much like the scales in courtrooms. The room was a great hall with rows of seats that could support about 100 people.

"Joseph," Dillie began. "The writing on the wall tells the story of Mars. Not many of us beings are living today who are old enough to remember Mars, at least when it was beautiful. They only know the arid red planet with its thin atmosphere. You may not believe this, but Mars was like this a little over 100 years ago."

This was fascinating news, but a little confusing at the same time. Even Lily seemed a little taken aback by the statement. I tried to remain expressionless, but Dillie managed to read my thoughts as her sinister smile managed to form in response to my confusion.

"Yes Joseph," Dillie remarked. The expression on her face became more serious. Dillie settled in as if she was about to tell a story. "Dworea was a lush planet with thick swaths of vegetation that was as red as a radish. We lived in paradise on our home planet. Work was a hobby, and there were virtually no problems. One day, all of our fellow beings gathered together for the yearly celebration and selections to Hughneir in the Zephnache Chie. Well, I was up for selection because of this new fruit that I had designed, Fenie. Fenie was a type of fruit on Dworea that was sweeter than a strawberry and packed more vitamin impact than a daily multivitamin. I designed this one day so that the fruit would taste the way your mind would want it to taste and provide whatever your body needed at the time. All the testing that I did on the fruit showed it to be harmless. Besides, there was so much of it and it grew so fast that there would never be another hungry mouth in the universe. I envisioned interplanetary ambassadors coming to receive some of the Fenie. Unfortunately, the Fenie is a slow killer. Within months, a few of the lore researchers noticed similarities between Fenie and another fruit that was forbidden from production. They ignored it because they could not understand why they would believe something was bad, but not documented thoroughly. The health researchers noticed the effects it had on sensitive groups, but never realized the subtle effects of health until it was too late. Because it became a staple of our diet, except for the most devoted to the lore or health, most beings were dead within a few years. Furthermore, planting Fenie began to be taxing on the planet. Farming it was poisonous to the surface and to the atmosphere. The planet was mostly inhabitable within a few months. The 'Mars' you see on your vessels today was the result of the destructive power of the Fenie on our planet. It was supposed to be the answer to a question that was never asked. We were never hungry. Our planet's resources always produced exactly what we needed. The Undefinable One that governs this universe most definitely judged Dworea for the worst. Fortunately, some were able to escape and a group of us landed in what is known as Area 51."

Lily spoke up at the moment that was presented.

"Martians who were captured at Area 51 were tortured because people are cruel and they thought we were hiding secrets of our technology from them. We flew here in a massive saucer to the middle of an uninhabited desert that would serve as the diplomacy grounds. We did not account for the hostility that immediately found itself upon us. As the more advanced race, we refrained from engaging as that would be the greater crime. We were also unprepared for the conditions that Earth and our human captors would subject us to in order to keep us in line. Our human captors tried to replicate everything we had: our language, biology, and technology. They tried to create it using their technology and the materials available from the resources on Earth. Humans are very intelligent beings but arrogant and impatient for results. There were only a handful of Martians who knew the secret of the technology. Martian loyalty is worth more than life or death. The technology was most important as humans are capable of abusing that power."

I looked a Dillie in her big brown eyes. She seemed very serious. I resisted the urge to ask her to continue on.

I rested on my arms for a moment. I looked intently at Dillie. I spoke carefully. "Dillie, I thank you for sharing that important bit of history with me. I hate to say that it will have no impact on my judgment today simply because I figured you had your reasons for doing what you did. However, you have helped me to gain some clarity in my thoughts and I know my verdict. Dillie, I find you guilty of conspiring against your people and committing treason by selling advanced Martian secrets with known fallen beings that may or may not have been exploited for technological and militaristic purposes. I recognized that you received money, which you claim to have donated in full to Martian well-being, but without an independent third party to verify your contributions to Martians, that information cannot be used to establish innocence or guilt."

I could see that Dillie's countenance had dropped significantly. I continued with my sentence. "However, considering your importance to the movement and how your death would make for a spectacle, I do not believe death is the answer. I propose that you resign from leadership, effective immediately, and recommend Lily as your interim successor until a true succession occurs in accordance with your laws. It will also help to have her lead, as she is the only one who knows what is happening with the humans and Martian technology. You will have no power to make decisions and your public retirement should serve as a message to those who will come after you."

When I finished my speech, Lily stood and said, "Very well, I agree with Joseph's verdict. We will have to agree on a limit to my term in the interim. Also, we need to prepare for damage control if they decide to tell the world about your decisions. In the meantime, Joseph, it may be appropriate for you to go back to your home."

The coldness with which she delivered her wishes and the complacent agreement offered by Dillie let me know that I had no chance in changing her mind. I felt the bell ringing, marking the end of my time here with the Martians. Leaving them left me feeling incomplete and hurting. "No closure," I whispered to myself over and over again as I packed up my belongings. It hurt to gather up my notes and the small trinkets that would forever remind me of the time I spent with the Martians.

The chilled New Mexican air when offloading from the plane gave me an unwelcoming breeze as I walked off the plane onto the tarmac. I spent my days going over every decision I made during the time I was at the compound. As my writing on the Martians evolved, so did my mind. Every day, something new was revealed to me about the far reaches of the universe when I observed the night's sky. I was overwhelmed with the amount of information in my mind.

Chapter 15

The heat from my childhood home was almost too much to bear. "I should have purchased those air conditioning units," I yelled to myself, as if I could will the units there. I stirred under the covers all night, sweat covering my body and a light headache reminding me that sleep was impossible. It was not just the impossible heat; I had been waking up out of my sleep for the past few weeks at exactly 2:30 am.

I had the same recurring nightmare of sorts where this man with large canine teeth was following me around. I caught myself in thought, I knew that man, he was Fien Dioni. I had seen him around town. Sometimes, I would be sitting in the café, but I was sure I was just resting in bed. Often, I would see some eyes peep over a newspaper, or a strong sense of anger and confusion would rise. I tried to suppress my frustration but it was hard to ignore. I sipped my coffee as I read the headline for the tabloids: *SCANDAL: MARTIAN CAPITOL IN TURMOIL? SOLE HUMAN ALLOWED ON INSIDE CAUSES STIR, SAYS MARTIAN INSIDER.*

I huffed audibly. "Who is behind this nonsense?" Was I asleep or awake? I could not tell anymore. All I knew was I needed a break from this whole Martian thing.

Walking around town was simple, as being a human granted me access pretty much anywhere with little to no questioning. I walked through a security checkpoint with little to no hassling. Martians, on the other hand, had to endure great privacy violations to just cross into the city. One Martian female was forced to strip down in view of all who dared to watch while the human gatekeeper searched her for weapons.

It all seemed so clinical as the gate keeper went through the motions of lifting her exposed breasts, having her spread her legs, running his fingers through her hair. Some muttered "whore" under their breath as they passed by. The Martian faced forward, enduring the humiliation with a forced pride. The sad reality behind all of it was the knowledge into the hearts of the people watching. I could sense the perverted joy at seeing this being violated in unimaginable ways.

Seeing that reminded me why I was doing this work. Most humans would never see it from my perspective, because most humans would never ask themselves if there was anything wrong. Also, the media spends its time slanting the stories so that Dworeans are considered the monsters, and the safety of humanity is at the mercy of the "extra-terrestrial terrorists." I muttered curses at humanity's cruelty under my breath as I continued towards the city.

I decided on breakfast and stopped at a local coffee shop, the Bean Machine Coffee Thing Café. I settled, because I could not remember the place my mother used to take me on special occasions for breakfast as a child so I could stir up the nostalgia from a previous life. I ordered a blueberry muffin and a hot-hot medium caramel deluxe mocha expresso with extra whipped cream. "The extra whipped cream is to counter the heat of the drink," I promised the barista, not really sure within myself as to why that was necessary. A result of my new mind, which questioned everything I did as an uninformed person.

They never really cared about my excuses, always keeping a happy expression and offering, "Thank you for your patronage, sir," after I took my drink. I looked around the crowded cafe and settled on a communal table with my back to the window.

As I sipped the drink, I considered the Martian movement and how their struggle would change the way future Martians live and interact with humans. I also considered how I may be viewed in Martian society and human society. Then I noticed that I was being watched by a man with a newspaper. The man seemed to be out of place, like a photograph with the focus moved to everything around the subject. I tried to look directly at the man, but could not make out his face. I thought to stand, but my body would not move. Just then, I realized that the restaurant was empty and I was sitting alone, across the way from the man. He got up and walked towards the door. I recognized him—it was Fien. The well dressed and broad-shouldered man opened the door and turned back to me with his contorted grin and said, "Well, are you coming?"

My body immediately moved into action, and I followed him into the street and down an alleyway before I realized what was happening. I knew he was coming. My mind was warning me. My heart was preparing me. And my soul was guiding me. I knew that this was something that needed to happen, and I was ready. I had a hard time sleeping and my body was not allowing me to eat much food. All of this leading up to the battle with Fien.

I stood outside the clay colored building, next to the air conditioning unit of the coffee shop. The air carried the fresh scent of freshly baked goods. The sky was gray; I breathed in some air to regain control. I stretched my neck to the left and right and hissed, "What do you want, you scoundrel?" I surprised myself with my level of agitation.

His jaw slightly dropped and he looked at me incredulously. "I am offended, aren't we better friends that that?" He asked this question in his usual tone of voice. That deep, slow drawl sent shivers down my spine. His face was more pronounced than usual. It was as if his teeth grew outside of his mouth. His eyes had a yellow tint under the red. I thought about flames when I looked into his eyes. He turned about face to saunter further into the alley. His nails were longer and sharper, and his hands were noticeably older as he scratched the wall of the alleyway we traversed, leaving behind marks. "Do not answer that, my feelings cannot handle the disappointment. Follow me Joseph."

I kept walking, falling in line behind my captor. My little mutiny had cost me all of my energy. My collar felt damp, and my hands were locked to my sides. I felt a strong wave of despair wash over my body and the terror inside my heart forcing its way out to the surface. Every ounce of my soul quivered as the hair follicles on Fien's head opened up to allow hair to sprout. Each one had a mind of its own, creeping towards me as the serpent to its helpless prey. I closed my eyes, certain I was dreaming, only to open them back into my circumstance. Accepting my fate, I changed the subject. "What are we doing?"

"Better," Fien's low growl barely audible through his speech. "We are here to negotiate. My employer realizes that you are a man of tremendous character. We came to you with an inappropriate proposition and want to remedy it."

I stumbled behind him, the invisible tether never allowing me to get more than 3 steps behind him. His pace forced me to keep moving, even with the needles in my feet.

We stopped, an abrupt end to our journey, at the dead end in the alley. I looked at the three walls, and asked, "Where are we and why here?"

Fien chuckled and snapped his finger. Two wooden chairs and a card table unfolded from nothing in the ground. "Sit, Joseph. We have much to discuss." I plunked onto the chair.

"Joseph, why are your shoulders slumped? Your chin is to your chest and your head is against the table. What have I done to you? Please, have some water." He smiled, waving his hands in a circle over the table, and the bottle materialized.

I stared in disbelief at the bottle. I wanted this to be a dream so badly. My mind was busy searching the cosmos for an answer. My eyes glossed over.

"Are you impressed? Ah, parlor trick, Joe. Magician never reveals his secret though." Fien's words echoed in my mind.

I lifted myself upright at the table. I was exhausted, but I managed to exhale, "Please talk so you can move on." I slumped my head closer to the table. I stared at the table, a helpless prisoner. Fien complied with my demand. "Very well." He pulled his chair out and sat while keeping his eyes focused on me. He rested his hands into one another, almost looking like a prayer, and began.

"As you may know, my client is eager to remove the nuisance of the Martian's call for human recognition with peace and while retaining their dignity. They are aliens, illegal aliens."

I knew he was calling for a reaction. Dillie was the same way, I did not take the bait. I asked, "That is not important to our discussion. What are you doing talking to me? And who is your leader?"

Fien winced, but caught himself quickly. He sat back in the chair, moving his arms to his lap. "We want you to go to the Martians. They trust you and will follow your direction. Say that you believe they should not pursue this any further. We heard that you might be counted as a judge among them. Say that you have considered the law and believe they should back down from their demands. We know their law, the judge can steer one's fellow beings in a direction."

My mind jolted; it knew the answer. As if my response was being spoken through me, I said, "The Martian law says a judge can dictate direction, but it ultimately must suit the greater moral tenet of loving others as oneself. By making such a declaration, I would be violating the principal tenet of Martian living. A judge cannot make declarations unless it raises the moral wellbeing of Martians. But I think you know that."

Fien's face expressed a mixture of admiration and annoyance. "Ah, Lily's stargazer seems to have grown. Please tell me, do you still dream of her?"

My face shaded slightly. "How could you know something like that?" I spat out the words before I could think, but I decided to let it go and leave. "Are we done?" I heaved my body upwards to get up from the table. My strength surprised me as it returned to my body. As if it was there all along, waiting for me to claim my rightful position as owner. Everything felt foreign. My body was numb, but I could control the movements.

As I made my exit from the table and out of the alley, I heard its voice. "Not yet Joseph, please allow his message, it's important."

I stopped. I was exhausted, and facing him would give away my advantage. I was not up for any more games. "Quickly," I hissed but remain faced away from him.

His voice retained its sinister growl, but lost its effect on me. "In the interest of fair play, my client thought it would be appropriate to alert you to our doings. We have discovered the Martian weakness, we will make a move very soon. If I may, I will give you a riddle to help you figure it out."

I felt this becoming more of a waste. I started walking away. The more I moved, the illusion began to fall. The wall of the alley began melting away, the familiar decor of the coffee shop began to form.

Just then, the apparition called out, "You will need to hear this. You may have agreed to not be in each other's lives, but your girlfriend is in danger."

I stopped in my tracks. The dream was fading. The walls of the dream alley were ripped and shredded like an old home with tattered wallpaper. "Continue," I ordered him.

In almost a rhythmic sonnet, Fien sang, "The souls of many; away like a mist. The secret to life; plants, fruits, or fish. The saboteur; an heir to the throne. Removing the joint; angels never known."

"What does that mean?" I did not intend to ask the question.

Fien chuckled, "Up to you to figure out. Hopefully you make it in time. But I will give you something else of interest. Your Martian girlfriend has an admirer, and the rivalry will commence. It seems miss Lily is as much a busy body as her predecessor."

I almost turned around to question him, but I resisted. "Okay, I will deal with that when the time comes." I walked out of the vision and back into the coffee shop. Surprisingly, I woke up in my seat.

"How long was I out?" I asked the woman who was staring at me.

She looked at me in surprise. "What are you talking about? You just sat down."

I accepted her statement and walked out with my drink. What happened to me? And why had no time passed by? What was Fien talking about in his riddle? I wondered what was going on with Lily.

I did not know how I would accomplish my mission, but I knew that I had work to do in Bowie.

Chapter 16

"You are going back to the Martian compound?" The question that slipped from Ben's lips and through the phone was intended to convey surprise, but I was certain he expected it. It could be my distrust of Dillie, but I had a feeling he was aware of what I planned to do.

"Ben, I have to go deal with something very important. I cannot explain myself except to say that I experienced something strange, and now I have a mystery to solve." I rifled through my drawers, looking for breathable fabrics to handle the DC area summer.

Ben must have known what I was doing. "You know summers in DC are not much different than in New Mexico, right? The heat is similar, it does not get as cold at night though. I suggest you pack some light layers just in case. How long do you plan on spending in the compound?"

I knew his question was coming, yet it caught me by surprise. "I do not know, I have not thought about it too much."

"Ah, a mysterious itinerary that lacks a defined timeline. This can create obstacles to progress. You do know that fortune favors the prepared mind, right? Why not take a break and get some coffee? Think about what you plan to do, I can talk it over if you need me." I could hear the sincerity in his voice. I felt a calmness fill me.

"You know Ben, you have always been a good friend to me. You were the first of the judges I saw at the institute and you seem to be the most warm and receptive of me." I stopped packing and sat on the bed. I looked at my childhood room.

It was a bare white wall except for a blue stripe that separated the bottom half of the wall from the top half. "Bears," I thought to myself, remembering the pattern hiding under the blue from when I was a child. I laid down on the old queen-sized bed, the smell of the sheets reminding me of my mother. My mind started to drift back to the conversation about my father. I thought of the last time I saw him and how he walked out on us. I allowed my mind to tarry there for a moment and closed my eyes. That moment was a second too long.

"Joseph," I heard Ben almost whisper. I heard him, but the damage was done, I knew what I needed to do and I had to do it soon.

My blood began to boil and soul panicked. I needed to leave. I threw everything I saw into the suitcase. I am certain I was prepared to stay for a month. "Ben, I must go now, I thank you for your words. I just wanted you to know what I was about to do."

"Very well," Ben accepted my decision. He did not offer another word of resistance.

I waited for a moment and hung up. I felt terrible for being rude, but I was going to be late. I called a taxi and headed to the airport.

The airport was more of an old road that some farmers paved to be a runway than a hub to service a population to and from certain locations. The room was a large warehouse with a few small jets scattered around, each with a mechanic and a pilot working on them, and a small room for waiting. I was able to afford joining a jet charter flight with Congresswoman Bonnie Wrait. She was flying to Washington D.C. and was thrilled to allow me a seat.

"Well, you sure are early. Why do you look so rushed?" The flight attendant at the desk near the entrance was looking at me in surprise. She wore a blue pantsuit and a white bandana around her neck. She looked to be in her late thirties. She took my license to confirm my identity. "You are 45 minutes early Mr. Vance."

I huffed, "A tardiness almost cost me the job I have, I will not make the same mistake twice." I took my identification back and walked to the waiting room. A professional's paradise was the thought that crossed my mind. High-end computers sat at the far corner of the room. Tablet computers and note taking pens and paper were neatly distributed about the room. Comfortable recliners peppered about with a small table. On top of the table was a cornucopia of coffee, assorted pastries, and a few jaw breaker candies. I could not resist the candy, so I grabbed a handful and slipped into a nap as I waited for my flight.

"Mr. Vance?" The attendant nervously approached me. You need to get up now, your flight is prepared to take off."

"Oh wow, I fell asleep but I forgot to set my alarm. Please forgive me." I gathered my things and quickly shuffled after her. As I boarded the plane, I could sense the excitement as to my whereabouts and felt a little ashamed and surprised that they did not see me in the waiting room.

The cabin of the plane was the plane I had only seen in movies. The interior was a mix of beige and wood. The cabin sat only ten people and everyone else had taken their seats. Two seats shared a comfortably large table that slid out along with the comforts of back massagers and enough outlets to stage a command center, if needed. I took the last seat available, in front of the Congresswoman.

"I made sure they left this seat open for you. It is nice to finally meet you Mr. Vance, I'm Bonnie Wrait." She extended her hand and held a genuine smile on her face. Her skin was pale, but not powdery white like her teeth. Her figure was slim, but not waif-ish. Her auburn hair counterbalanced the fire in her brown eyes, forcing me to linger on them a little to long. She wore a black knit blouse with white jeans, and some shiny black flats. She looked no older than mid-forties.

"Nice to meet you Bonnie, my name is Joseph. Thank you for allowing me to fly with you to Washington." I placed the web of my hand into hers. A firm handshake technique that I learned from Ben.

Bonnie sat back into her chair and folded her arms over one another. Her eyes stared at me over her reading glasses. She tapped her fingers against one another a few times. "Joseph," she said as she leaned forward with her hands on the slide out table, "why help the Martians?"

I stopped and thought for a moment, "I do not know, I guess the same reason you chose the conservative party. I believe in their cause."

Bonnie chuckled at that notion. "Politics is never that simple, I did what I had to do in order to get elected. Well not true, I believe in the overarching mission that the conservative party espouses. However, I do not align with everything. I also wanted to be the person who was in a position to make a difference. That is why I chose my path. Now tell me why you chose yours."

"I chose to work with the Martians because that was around the time my dad left. I am not upset with him over leaving, I am hurt that I do not really know why. I guess I hoped to find out something about the Martians that will tell me that he left for a good reason. Or maybe I am doing this to remind me of him since their appearance was the last time I ever saw him. It is so simple, but that is my deep-down explanation for the great noble mission that has caused so much ruckus." My confession dripped from my lips like the overflow of a waterfall, surprising me with my mental consciousness's insight.

She was leaning in, focused on me. Her hands were in prayer under her chin. Her ruby red lips pursed and her slender nose scrunched. "I believe you, but I do not want to believe. Every word that comes out of your mouth seems so precise. It is as if you have rehearsed everything you said a few seconds before you say it. Almost as if you have a complete understanding of the world around you. You would make an incredible politician. I bet you would make for a more interesting partner."

My eyes grew wide, but retreated back to their normal state to disguise my shame. "I am a little surprised at your statement. Are you attracted to me?"

Bonnie cackled. "I would love to explore that possibility, but I am sure your heart is with someone else. Your 'Rosa Sharon' is out there waiting, but not for long I hear. Anyway, it would be political suicide to be affiliated with a Martian sympathizer."

I was a little offended. "What does that mean? I am seeking equality for all. I sympathize with all beings in existence, it just happens to be that Martians have it the worst right now."

She switched her convivial nature for a more reserved countenance. "I meant nothing by it. It is all about optics for me. I have no problem with Martian recognition, I just don't think we should extend them citizenship and a full cadre of rights as a result. We treat them like honored guests on this planet as we would treat any other human from another country. We have wronged them, this planet is not their home, and we cannot send them home. Can you see how difficult of a predicament we are trying to navigate? Someone is not your friend, but they show up to your house, would you let them live there?"

My reaction to her statement was one of bewilderment. She must have noticed, because she quickly offered, "Joseph, your positions pose no problem for me personally, but my base of supporters is a lot more extreme than me. I was trying to say a perceived union with you would not look good, no offense. Besides, I have ambitions and desires that do not fit a family into it. I am selfish; I like to do what I want, when I want to do it, with whomever I feel like doing it with; wherever it pleases me to do it, however I envision it."

"None taken," I lied. I knew what her intentions were, and I refused to get caught up by saying something that could go back to the public. Dillie was a master at teasing reactions out of seemingly innocuous statements. I was better prepared for questioning of this sort. I was unsure of what she wanted, but I would not allow myself the stress of being caught in a scheme. "You also do have a good point; a single person is better equipped to fully devote oneself to a purpose."

"Good, Joseph, now let us talk about your business while we rush to get to Washington. What is going on? You paid a lot of money to join us on this flight and your urgency to get there suggests some excitement. What is happening?" Bonnie was engaged, preparing to hear some gossip as if we were old friends talking.

I contemplated giving her some information on the riddle, but I thought the better of it. I remembered whose side she was on. "I have some unfinished interviews on the Martian ethical dichotomy to finish up. I also need to take a few photos."

"Right." Her fingers on the right hand pinched the edge of her glasses and peeled them off. "Well, since it is obvious you do not trust me, let me put myself out there. Is this about the mysterious disappearance of the Martian being James Coswell?"

"What?" I caught myself in thought and added a leading question. "What would make you think the leader of the Martian biological organization is missing and not on leave or extended break?" I had hoped she would have taken the bait.

Bonnie either ignored my trick or my trap was more cunning than I at first thought, "Joseph, I hope you realize the United States government has been tapping into the Martian compound since it was built. We have insiders and regular correspondence with Martian leadership."

"They are tapping the Martian phones? Well, are the Martians speaking English?" I thought about it, but thought against admitting that humans could not sense Martian groaning.

"Yes, they were." I could see her mind working while she stretched out that statement. "Can I tell you something if you tell me something?" I hesitated, but nodded for her to continue. "The latest intelligence committee meeting revealed nothing of substance on the plans of the Martians. But we did find out something odd. Your name came up in some documents from the Martian computer archives. They discussed you and whether your presence would cause problems and draw your father out of hiding?"

My heart stopped. My father? He was alive? I had not seen him. How did Lily and Dillie know? So many questions about who he was and what he was doing today raced through my mind. Why did he leave? I could not imagine how my facial expression displayed the shock on my face. I was sure my jaw dropped. "What does my father have to do with anything?"

Bonnie smirked and wagged her finger, "No sir, your turn." She placed both her fists under her chin and her eager demeanor waited for my story.

I thought for ten seconds and considered what story would pose the least disastrous results if I divulged. "I am headed to Maryland to solve a mystery. I think Dillie's leadership is being challenged."

Bonnie leaned in further, her interest piqued.

"Nothing more, I have told you too much." I considered the look on her face: a playful puckered lip and her eyes staring into mine. I pretended to cave. Okay, this will be it." I stopped myself again.

Her eyes widen and a smile crossed her face. Bonnie offered me a playful punch to my arm. "Please tell me, please, please, please," She grabbed my hand and kissed it three times. She cupped my left hand into hers and placed it against her chest. "Feel my heart racing Joseph!" Someone who observed us might have assumed we were lovers, even I had a hard time distinguishing.

I looked around the cabin, but no one was paying us any attention. I thought of my tell; I needed something strong, yet meaningless. I leaned in close to her right ear. I whispered, "Martians do not speak English to one another. They have their own language. If you want to find out their real secrets, translate that language; that is, if you ever get a chance to hear it." Humans would never be capable of translating Martian speech because we could not hear its frequency.

Bonnie sat contemplating the information I gave her for the duration of the flight while I considered my own mysteries.

As we were walking off the plane, Bonnie tapped me on the shoulder and said, "I am not finished with you, we are going to talk about that 'revelation' soon." With that, Bonnie grabbed my shirt and gave me a peck on the lips, one of her legs raised like long lost lovers. After a few seconds, the kiss ended and she buried her head into my chest. She then raised her head and whispered in my ear, "We would make great partners, all it takes is a change of stance. Or, we could even have something in secret."

"Not likely," I retorted quietly with as kind of a smile I could muster, "no offense."

She faked another smile, perpetuating the illusion that we were lovers having a private conversation. "Very well, I know you are an honest man. However, do not let the Martians destroy your chances at a properly yoked relationship."

I tried to correct her. "Our political differences do not have any impact on us being together..."

She raised her shushing finger to my lips, "I know, I wasn't talking about all of them. Just one Martian in particular." With that, she flipped her hair in my face and walked away.

I looked up, and her staff as well as other plane guests had surprised and scandalous looks for a few moments. I gathered my things and considered Bonnie's words until I got to the Martian Compound.

Chapter 17

The cozy yet spacious office space for Lily held a special place in the being's heart. Lily sat in her cushioned leather chair and admired the handiwork of her fellow beings in putting together a desk out of trees. Some of the drawers were uneven but Lily appreciated the familiarity of her desk and would never ask to upgrade. Looking at the outfit hanging on the rack, Lily wondered if she should change into a more flattering outfit. She believed in looking her best and she felt out of place in her jeans and t-shirt.

Lily pored over the list of Martian needs that were not being met and considered how to care for them. "No one is going to be happy with the arrangements," Lily muttered to herself, "how did Dillie do it?"

Just then, a knock came at the door and the guest chose to enter without invitation. "Dr. Ryemore," Lily peeked above the document she was reading towards the Martian standing in her doorway. "What can I do for you?" Her irritation came off much more pronounced than she intended.

"Jacob, please meet Dr. Crocus, who is hereinafter know as Lily. I know we are on better terms than the formality you offer now." The Martian took off his designer blazer and hung it on the coat rack, disturbing the outfit that Lily hung on it earlier.

"Well dressed, even on hot days Jacob." Lily admired him from head to toe. He wore some large round glasses frames, a shiny cream-colored button-up shirt, a blue bow-tie with red polka dots, with suspenders that matched his tie, holding up his red pants, and finished with some navy loafers. "You make my black jeans and blue t-shirt seem less fashionable. Now, what can I do for you?"

"You are all business, very well. I have completed preliminary studies of the sick Martians and I believe I have detected a trend." Jacob stood in place and did not say anything else.

Lily placed the stack of papers onto her desk and looked up at Jacob. "Will you please tell me what is going on? I do not have an appetite for this dramatic game right now."

Jacob scowled, but tempered his frustration and slowly said, "Lily, this is serious. This is not a game. My studies have concluded that these Martians will die. There is no chance, even if we can get a cure. Their bodies have deteriorated so much and so fast that I am doing everything I can to make them comfortable."

Lily stood at the desk. "I cannot believe this is happening. Tell me everything you know so far. I want to know the little things, even your conjectures."

Jacob huffed. "We have three patients in the hospital. They are experiencing severe vomiting and diarrhea. I have managed to treat those symptoms by feeding them dry foods and keeping them properly hydrated. They have also complained about feeling like their insides are on fire. Mobility is not a problem for them, but quarantine was necessary to get a grip on the magnitude of the disease. It may be contagious, and others will probably start experiencing symptoms."

Lily started pacing the room. "Do we know who is at risk? Where does it come from? Martians have not been sick since we left our home, how is his possible?" She folded her arms one over another. "Weeks after taking the lead and our beings are in crisis."

Jacob walked over and grabbed Lily's shoulders. They stared at one another. "Lily, I do not know who is at risk, but the worst thing we can do right now is panic. It is difficult to trace viruses and I doubt we will truly know where any of this came from. I do have my theories. We are also living in a fallen world, maybe that has something to do with our troubles. Right now, we should be vigilant and keep in mind that there may be some who mean us harm."

Lily looked at the floor. "You mean the humans?"

"Yes, I do Lily." Jacob removed his hands from Lily's shoulders and walked to the windows. He placed his hands behind his back. "They imprisoned us although we came in peace. They enslaved us to get what they could not conjure themselves. They take what does not belong to them and despise us for being better than them. Their planes, their cell phones, their every advanced technology came from Martian mind and back. Parasites, the lot of them. I put nothing past them and this is probably to rid us for good." Jacob slapped the desk when he said good, startling Lily.

Lily shook her head. "I do not believe the humans would do this. At least, not as a collective unit. Not all of them monsters. We are making headway."

Jacob interrupted Lily. "Maybe we are making progress, but do not forget who enslaved us. I like your optimism, but we have to pay close attention to what is the obvious answer. Maybe that human Joseph has something to do with this."

Lily's mouth fell open a little as she expressed her shock, "Oh." Her hand went over her mouth as to shut herself up from saying more.

"You were about to defend him?" Jacob focused on her face, intent on deriving the truth from her eyes. "He is the only human who was allowed great access to our resources and history. What if he has used that against us? How can you defend him?"

Lily turned her back to Jacob, carefully considering how she might answer him. "I am not, Joseph does not seem like the type to betray."

"It doesn't matter," Jacob retorted. "Look at what he is doing. The news is on fire with images of Joseph kissing Bonnie Wrait, they are dating one another."

Lily coughed, almost choking on her own spit. "How could he?"

Jacob ran to Lily's back. "Are you okay? She is an adversary to us, but this news seems to have hit you hard."

Lily caught her breath, "Yes, I am fine. I was surprised that someone who is our ally would be so careless as to allow a person to be so close to him, who is against us like Bonnie." Lily shocked herself with her ease and wiliness to lie, but she needed to know more without raising the suspicion of the Martian public. She made a mental note to ask Joseph about this when they met again. "What are we going to do about the sick Martians?

"Let me handle them for now." He turned towards the door and said on his way out, "Lily, it may not be the most appropriate time for this, but let us get together for dinner soon. I would like to know more about what is going through your mind."

"Okay," Lily squeaked out with all the sweetness she could muster. She looked around the desk and grabbed her notebook. She ran down the darkened hallways, filled with the mural of Martian history. She reflected on the beautiful deep red of its images and wondered what home would be like if it was habitable. She turned the corner, flailing as she blasted through the assorted wet papers hanging from the ceiling of the mystery being called Dillie. "Why are you constantly sitting on the floor when I walk into your office? Do you know that you have a desk?"

Dillie uncrossed her legs and stood up, shaking a little, showing off her age or the effect of stress. She wore grey shorts and a tank top, surprising Lily as Dillie was usually more colorful.

"It is impolite to interrupt an elder Martian." Dillie mimicked her speech after an old human female, "Are you coming because your boyfriend has found a female more willing?"

Lily felt heat flash through her system. "How did you know? No, that is not why I am here." Lily offered her plea to Dillie unconvinced of her own conviction.

"Lily, I can see through you. I can see through most beings. It is my gift and curse, but you already know that about me. And none of that matters, I know you care for him. Do not egg him on, okay?" Dillie's face feigned concern until her wicked scowl returned as she said in her normal voice, "I may want to give it a try!"

Lily's face turned a slight rose color. She clinched her fists.

"It seems that you do not take this lightly. Maybe I should stop joking?" Dillie stopped and looked at Lily with a warm smile. "I am sorry, friends?" Dillie extended her right hand.

Lily raised her hand slowly, "Okay, friends. What is going on, why are you wearing grey?"

"I woke up this morning and did not feel right in my soul, so I wore the color of anticipation. It is not white or black, so I am unsure what will happen. Why did you come, Lily? Has something happened?" Dillie's expression of concern culminated with what could become tears.

She took a deep breath and continued on, "A few Martians have turned up really sick. They are clearly on a path to death. Dr. Ryemore is working through this crisis, but we are unsure of why this is happening. He thinks it may be humans. I am not so sure."

"The fall." Dillie looked at the floor. "I had a feeling that something like this was going to happen. I did not think it would be so soon. We are becoming fallen."

Lily was bewildered. "How do you mean?"

"We never got sick until now. If this is happening, then we are in grave danger. I must go." Dillie ran to her closet and grabbed a suitcase, throwing everything she saw in the closet into the bag. Dillie did not distinguish any type of clothes, instead chucking everything into the bag as if it was trash.

"Dillie, I need you to explain what you are talking about. Are we in danger?"

Dillie filled her bag to the brim and closed it tight. "I wish I could explain it to you, but it is too difficult." Dillie ran to a bookshelf near the edge of the room. "R-, Re-, Resistance 'Abalam Shaduam.' One of our foremost judges. Here it is and I will give it to you."

Lily took a step back, "His real name? They are listening to us now."

Dillie blew the dust off the book. "I am certain they cannot hear it. This was written some few hundred years ago by a Martian who was obsessed with the end of our existence. He had almost a prophetic knowledge of the circumstance that would lead to our departure from our home. He also wrote on the humans and how their world was not an option for our settlement. Read about his strange interaction with the master of Earth."

Lily took the book from Dillie's hand. "So, you are going to leave without telling me anything?"

Dillie looked into Lily's face with a grave expression. "I know you may think this is a game coming from me, but it is better that you do not know. The only thing I can tell you is you are safer not knowing and I can better control the flow of information if it only comes from me. I am not the leader of the Martians anymore, you are. Lead them, tell them as little as you can tell them in order to keep them out of your business and happy as they continue to live out their existences. Discern the person you can trust and keep everyone else out. Also, things may not always be as they seem. I must go."

Dillie gave Lily a hug and then left.

Lily was left standing in the middle of Dillie's office with the book in her hand. "What is happening?" Lily gazed at the book and wondered what to do next. A moment later, Dillie's phone ringed. Lily picked up the receiver. "Lily speaking, Dillie has just departed town, what can I do for you?"

"Oh? Lily? Hi, I just tried calling your office. I have a human, Joseph Vance, here to see you. He tells me that it is urgent. Shall I show him to your office or Dillie's office?"

Lily sighed, not prepared to engage Joseph at the moment. "Show him to Dillie's office. I will be waiting."

Chapter 18

Stepping onto the familiar campus of the Martian compound in Bowie, Maryland gave me the same warm feeling as coming home from a long trip. I recalled how much had happened in those fateful days where Dillie and Lily locked themselves in a struggle for ultimate power over the Martian beings' future. I laughed to myself at the absurdity of it all now that Lily was leading the Martians and they had decided to forgo their own happiness for the sake of the stress of the struggle for Martian equality. I regretted not doing more, not pursuing my heart, not casting all reservations aside for a taste of knowing what it would be like for us to love one another in that special way. I knew that I made the right decision but my "what if" left so much to be seen.

"Hey Joseph," exclaimed a Martian that I did not recognize. I nodded my head as I continued to the office building where she was located. I was surprised as to the infrastructure progress that had been made since Lily took charge. The grounds were better kept and the grass appeared a bit greener. I also could tell the roads were re-paved and gave the city center a new sense of life.

After chatting with the secretary and watching her fluster with nervousness as she scrambled to locate Lily, who was in Dillie's office, I walked that way.

Seeing Lily again after this month felt like a wave of calm warm ocean water hitting my body on a perfect day with a slight breeze. She walked down the hallway towards me with a smile reserved for friends and I half expected the fondest of hugs. Her outfit was not her normal garb, but she looked stunning in her jeans and t-shirt. "Gee, you are so beautiful!" My only offering to her fell flat.

She offered her hand to shake and said, "Joseph, it is good to see you as well. Come on in to Dillie's office." She motioned me into the door of Dillie's office where we once eavesdropped on an aware Dillie.

"What are we doing here, Lily? And where is Dillie? Has something happened?" I shot off a flurry of questions, not intending for her to be flustered.

Lily turned to me, betraying a look of shock. "I am not sure, she left without an explanation. But it has something to do with our fellow beings getting sick and dying."

"The souls of many; away like a mist." The words reverberated from my lips before I could trap them inside, echoing in my mind as my fears were confirmed.

"The what?" Lily seemed more confused and remained focused on me for my story.

I sat down and explained the vision with Fien and what he told me. I told her about the previous experience with him and how it came into fruition with Dillie. I gave her the rest of the riddle and the insight he seemed to have into our private lives. I was uncertain how he appeared only in my dreams, but I assumed there was some level of hypnosis and psychological suggestion.

"Before we came to Earth, Dillie and some of the other leaders disagreed on whether to come here. They always used to say there was a 'darkness descended on this planet.' I can see why they would think that if this is your experience." Lily slouched into Dillie's chair and thought for a few minutes.

I walked to the couch and stood before it in a daze of recall. The ancient knowledge of the Martians did not have much on this, but I could understand the agony that went into this decision. Earth was their last choice, they were desperate when they came here. Falleness was not contagious, but Martians were susceptible. "Yes, but we must figure out the rest. 'The secret to life; plants, fruits, or fish. The saboteur; an heir to the throne. Removing the joint; angels never known.' Any thoughts?"

"No idea, I have to discuss further with Doctor Ryemore." She stood up from Dillie's chair and made her way to the door. She held it open, signaling it was time for me to leave.

I remained seated on the couch. "How can I help?" When I asked, I began making my way out.

"No thank you, Joseph. I do not need any help from you and I am sure your ultimate allegiance is with humanity." Lily motioned me to go through the door and leave.

I felt the flutter in my gut that was akin to a low blow. "Not fair," but my mind stopped me before I could protest more and offered clarity. "Ah, I see. You have heard about Bonnie. It was nothing except an opportunistic photo opportunity. I am too polite to reject her in public. I will continue to think on the riddle. You can find me at the hotel down the street should you need anything." I walked out of the room and turned to her one more time. "Also, I know you have tracked down my father."

Lily's eyes widen and her face shaded darker green. She was always so easily flustered. I thought about what she must have hidden from me. Then her eyes narrowed. "It is not what you think, Joseph."

"That is all you can offer? I have not seen my father since I was a kid. Can you tell me where he is?" I asked my mind for the conscious answer, but it told me that I was not ready to hear it. My unexpected request had taken her by a surprise a little, but it also eased her somewhat. I could not quite put my finger on it, but she seemed relieved after I asked about his whereabouts.

Lily pulled out a slip of paper from a folder on Dillie's desk and handed it to me. "I have a local address, but I have not vetted it. You can have it if you want, but keep an open mind." She closed the door to Dillie's office and walked away from me.

Chapter 19

The address was1385 Reflections Cove. "How appropriate," I muttered to myself as I contemplated not going to speak to my father. I wondered why he did not reach out to me. Would he want to see me? Did I want to see him? Questions I pondered for too long on the drive over. No wonder I did not park in the driveway, I was terrified to face the man who walked out on me when I was too young to care for myself. The only memory I had of him was as my guardian.

I rapped the door three times and waited for an answer. I dreaded the interaction that we would have in a moment. Mainly, I feared getting closure.

A tall Persian woman with long brown hair opened the door. About the age I assumed my father would be, she was attractive in all respects. Much more so than I can remember my mother being. I resented my father even more at her sight.

"Hello, I am sorry to drop by unexpectedly, but my name is Joseph Vance and I am here..."

Before I could finish my sentence, the woman squealed with delight and gave me a hug. "Thank God you are here." She kissed me on each cheek a handful of times and hugged me again. "I did not think I would ever get the chance to meet you. Please come in, you must have so many questions. Josiah is inside and I know he will be eager to see you. He has not stopped talking of you since we married. My name is Shima."

Shock rippled through my soul at my father's nerve to remarry and start a new life, but my newfound stepmother was too kind for me to resent her. I did not know whether to believe her statement and this welcoming reception. She sucked the righteous indignation from the fires of my chest with the smallest of gestures, a hug.

We tarried too slowly for my anxiety, towards the living area. She held my hand the whole way despite my overt attempts to recover it. She managed to vomit out their life stories in the 30 second walk to the living area. I learned they had two children and met about year after my father would have left my family. I wondered if she knew that he was still married to my mother when he left and would have been freed only after she died about three years ago.

I sat on the couch and stared at the wall full of family photos that I never took. The signs of wealth accumulated were beyond impressive. She had a pet name for him, 'esgham,' which I ascertained was Persian for 'my love.' She brought two cups of tea with honey and sat them in front of me on the table.

And then he walked into the room. A strong man who was not lacking in size or height, his beard stretched to the middle of his chest and he looked at me and smiled. "Joseph, it is so wonderful to see you. I never thought this day would come. Are you well? Is there anything else I can get for you?"

This man, who left me as a child while my mother and I struggled to live. Now he stood here happy and content with his life? He seemed warm and kind. I hated him for leaving. I hated my mother even more for allowing him to go and not taking me. I reverted back to my days as a child and wanted daddy to approve of me. "I want nothing from you." I tried to not make it negative, but it came out angry.

His expression changed from that of joy to concern. "Is everything okay, Joseph? How is Angie?"

It burned my soul when he said her name. I considered lashing out at him and blaming him for her weak state, but I knew better than to not honor him with reason. "She passed a few years ago, it still hurts."

His eyes turned red and started to tear up. "I am so sorry Joseph. I wanted to apologize to her for everything, but I was too afraid to face her and my sins. She exposed me for the monster that I was and I could not stop myself." He buried his face into his hands and started sobbing.

I sat there with him, silent. The soul wrapped by my flesh cried out in pain with him. My senses threatened to move me and warned me that Josiah was a man wracked with guilt. I felt his pain as if it was my own, years of unsaid words and memories of wrongdoing.

Josiah rose from his hands with tear-soaked eyes. He said, "You know, I started a successful computer business when I left her. I got married to my soul equal. She gave birth to two girls, whom I loved more than my life. These three have softened my heart."

"What about your wife? Did you ever tell Shima about that? Did you ever mention 'Angie?'" I spouted her name sarcastically and I felt horrible because I knew she meant more to us than that.

Josiah hung his head. "Not initially. Shima knew me, but I did not let her in at first. I relished my independence and tried to exploit her, like I did Angie, in my new freedom. It was hell at night trying to sleep with all of the bad memories. But she ripped me from the shadows and made me come clean. She gave birth to our daughter, Grace, and demanded my bare soul or she would leave. I loved my baby girl and divulged the full extent of my sins. The conversation freed me truly, I realized

I was forgiven. As a result, my wife gave me Mercie, our second little girl."

I was drowning in the deep despair of his life. What had this man endured over the years?

"I knew then that I never loved Angie. I was cruel and harsh to her. Treated her like she was an animal. I was disappointed with my life and I searched for excuses to leave. I was a monster." He kept his face looking at me.

My consciousness advised me again, 'A man who faces his demons head on deserves the fullest grace.' Josiah regretted his bad decisions, but there was no need to punish him for something he had achieved closure on. I felt bad for my mother, but knew that she would not have held a grudge.

"What was Angie like after I left?"

I looked at him and said, "She was at peace. I could tell your departure caused her sadness, but she lived in solitude a lot happier than I think she might have been with you." I wanted to be delicate, but I knew sparing his feelings would remove my honesty. "Can you tell me why you would leave us? I am still your son."

His expression changed from jovial to confused and settled on a sad face. "She didn't tell you, did she?" I shook my head no. He began laughing and slapped his knee. "Figures she would do something like this to me. You got caught in the middle. I guess I deserve this because I was the one who left. Joseph...I am not your biological father."

That was it. I sank into my seat and the living room became infinitely larger. The room started to move and I could not control my body long enough to relax. I hated him, I did not know who I hated, but I hated him. I felt nauseous. My voice trembled as I weakly squeaked out, "How?"

"Seven months. I swore the baby was premature, but the doctors told me differently. Angeline kept doctoring the timeline, making me think I was crazy, but none of that mattered to me. I was having a son." What he delivered next was a shocking tale of how he was in an accident at work the day she admitted to an affair, which he did not believe because she said it was with an alien. He was in and out for a few weeks on pain medication. As soon as he was healed, she kept insisting they have sex and did other things to create a baby. He went with it. But something was always off about how quick I was born. No one else seemed to notice, especially not Angeline. He also observed that I only favored my mother, but never received any indication that another man came into the picture.

After he unloaded his story, I felt a sense of relief at the closure I was offered from a man who was never there. I also sort of lost myself in the revelation that I might be the spawn of a Martian. That seemed impossible and farfetched.

"You know, Joseph," Josiah offered, "I always sort of knew you were not mine. I did not want to believe it. It is fitting that she decided to have me tell you the story, a bit of a last-ditch effort to return the favor for my sins. I am sorry that you had to find out through me."

I stared at the floor for a long time. I was conflicted. "How can I be angry at you? I hated you for my life, but I am thankful that you did not stay and hurt me like you hurt my mother, despite her sins. Thank you."

I could tell that my statement offended him, but he accepted it. In my heart, I did not hate him anymore and wished him a good life. As I walked back to my car, I accepted the fact that I would never see the man I assumed to be my

father for my whole life. I forgave his sins against my mother
and me and prepared to move on. A true mission stood before
me as I sought to save the Dworeans from whatever threat they
had encountered. I left my father's house left me with so many
questions and I could not answer them on the drive home.

Chapter 20

I left Josiah's home in an emotional quandary and retreated back to my contemporary hotel near the compound to stay in for the time being. It was a comfortable but minimalistic bedroom. The anguish inside my heart from not having closure from my mother was too much to bear. I searched my mind for the secrets held within. My soul cried to God for an answer. And then I began my reflection.

I looked out the window and thought to myself about what was next. I remembered that I needed to solve the riddle. "The secret to life; plants, fruits, or fish. The saboteur; an heir to the throne. Removing the joint; angels never known." Saying it over and over in my mind, I thought about what I was missing and then I heard a knock at my door.

I approached the door with as quiet footsteps as I could manage. Three knocks pounded against the door, startling me backwards audibly. I opened the door to find Bonnie. She held two glasses with a bottle of wine and a smile. "What business could you have with me, Bonnie?"

"Olive branch?" She kept smiling, awaiting an invitation to come inside. "Come on Joseph, just one drink?"

I did not want to let her in my room, but something inside me entertained the thoughts. Maybe it was because I gazed at her frame a little too long. The way her clothes fit and the sneaky smile on her face gave way to an acceptance of her into my room.

"Please come in, Bonnie, but just one drink."

She cheered and did a heel click before she zipped through the door. We sat and both drank a full glass of wine before the conversation slipped from pleasantries. Bonnie was in the middle of a thought on her Sophomore year of college when I finally stopped her by asking, "What are we doing here Bonnie?"

"Okay Joseph, let us talk for real." She poured another glass and sipped before she leaned back into her chair and talked to me. "You are here at this hotel and not at the compound. Can I assume that not all is well?"

I was not sure if I should answer, so I remained silent for a few moments. Taking a few more sips the wine and then I decided to be honest. "Everything is at the moment. I am not there because they have Martian business to attend."

"Exactly, Martian business." Bonnie perked up and sat on the bed next to me. She grabbed my arm and leaned on me. "Joseph, I know you are interested in caring for the Martians, but their ultimate allegiance is to one another. Not to you. They have secrets Joseph, big secrets that go beyond tracking your father."

It could have been the feeling of rejection from Lily or the alcohol speaking, but I was beginning to agree with her. "And you know these secrets?" I did not mean to ask it as a question, but it felt like the thoughts were being fed to my mind.

"I know people who are paid a lot of money to know these things. They have told us that Martians communicate in a secret language. They also know about your dates with Lily. They know about the technology and how Dillie was holding back. They know that you know about it and your involvement in appointing Lily as the interim leader." Then her eyes went blank for a moment and she said, "And we know about the ceremony. What are you?" She blinked and continued drinking.

"What?" I assumed I drank too much and was a little drunk. I put my wine down and started gathering Bonnie's belongings. I needed to rest and would not be able to with her around me. "Look Bonnie, I am tired. Can we do this another day?" And that was the end of my conversation. I handed her effects over and shooed her to the door. She did not offer any rebuttals until we were standing on either side of the doors threshold.

"Can I stay until I sober up? You would not want anything bad to happen to me. Would you?" She puckered her lips and I thought of how she would be more annoying sober.

I said, "No way. I will pay for a hotel room, but you cannot stay here any longer." She walked away and did not look back. I felt bad, so I watched her walk to the elevator. The haze cleared up a few minutes later and I sobered up quickly. And then I collapsed on the bed and thought on what Bonnie had told me. What happened to her? I felt a subtle tug while she was in the room, but her removal took the tug with her. Laying in my bed, I thought of Lily most of the night. I wondered what I might be able to do to help.

Chapter 21

Just then another knock rattled me from my rest. My mind cursed wildly at the notion of Bonnie bothering me again. "Sorry," I yelled. "I am not interested in anything you have to offer me."

A loud, shrill laugh came from the other side of the door, rattling my bones. "Well, that is good, we have nothing to offer." Dillie's familiar voice rang into my ears and I hurried to open the door, fearing that someone may discover her.

"What are you doing here?" As I opened the door, I beheld Dillie and some other being in hooded cloaks. I almost let out a chuckle at the ridiculous sight of them. They had to know they were not fooling anyone. I stared at both of them as they entered my room and removed their cloaks. My eyes widened to see another Martian around Dillie's age. "There is another Martian as old as you?"

The other Martian look at me, he looked worn. His eyes were red and his body so frail that he shook every time he moved. "Your host is rude and in his underwear. He is not prepared for our visit." I looked down to realize that I was in my underwear and retreated to the bathroom with some pants in tow. "My name is James. James Coswell by the way." His voice carried a slight British twang.

Upon my return, Dillie slapped her knee in glee to the embarrassment I had endured. Then she ran to me and gave me a hug. "It is good to see you again, Joseph. I hope all is well." This hug seemed genuine. I acknowledged in my mind this as a rarity for Dillie and allowed myself to be moved at her kindness. However, in true Dillie fashion, she had to take away from the tender moment by asking, "Can we order some pizza?"

I ordered some food as James and Dillie argued about the benefits of consuming pizza. They settled on separate meals and I had the delivery company pick up some fruit on the way. We sat, and I caught Dillie and James up on what happened while I was in New Mexico. They asked about a place called Corona, but I was not familiar with it outside of the Roswell thing. The food came and we all ate, preparing for the difficult conversation that would come next. The discomfort loomed as Dillie took slow bites consuming most of the large pizza we shared by herself.

Once that was over, James began. "So, you have been approached by a suspicious entity who has malicious intent for us Martians? I do not think this a coincidence that this 'Fien' approached you with a riddle. Dillie told me that she has never seen him, but interacted with him and he carried a level of sinister that made her shudder."

I saw that Dillie told James about the dealings with Fien. James seemed detached, or perhaps unbothered, by the circumstances of her interactions with Fien. He also could have not known the full extent of her treachery. I made eye contact with Dillie, hoping to mentally convey to her the importance of telling him. She just smiled back.

James looked me over once again. "Do not mind her, I am well aware of her deeds and misdeeds. We are equals, hiding nothing from one another." The old Martian walked over to me. "But you are most interesting indeed. I knew Dillie trusted you, but I did not realize what you are until now." He had placed his hands all over my person. He was studying my face, pinching my cheeks and opening my eyes wide. "As the Great

Martian Physician, I have the ability to understand biological phenomena." He then opened my mouth wide and looked into my throat. I heard a reaction of shock and the old Martian stumbled back. He looked at me and then turned to Dillie, speaking in their native tongue.

They argued. My mind could not unpack everything they said as the culmination of my ancient Martian knowledge was incomplete. I learned new things everyday. The knowledge of the ancients and the expanded universe was almost infinite. But they were talking about something I could not quite grasp. They discussed me and my origins, questioning how I could have attained the ability to communicate Martian. I was not sure whether or not I should speak. Dillie facial expression confirmed as such when she continually looked to me, commanding via telepathy that I should not speak. I refused to comply and blurted out in English, "I think it was that ceremony that Dillie performed."

James turned to me in shock. "You have the ancient knowledge?" His countenance shifted to anger and then to despair. Dillie grabbed James's shoulder and whispered something in his ear. "I see that something has happened and you have this gift. I was a little taken aback at your understanding, because the transference is almost impossible for humans." He turned to look at Dillie, who nodded in agreement. He turned back to me, "No, I cannot lie Joseph, it is impossible. We must find John." James began to berate Dillie over her decision-making again. It was hard to make out all of the words because I think they switched to a more obscure dialect of Martian. I could tell that because my mind started unpacking the language and the meaning behind the words. The traditions unfolded in my mind and started unloading quicker than I could think. It hurt so much that I had to close my ears and eyes to allow my mind time to digest what it was unpacking. I was able to quiet the information transmission after a few minutes.

When I removed my hands from my ears and opened my eyes, I heard James say, "As I thought, his conversion is incomplete. Ascension from fallenness does not appear to be as quick as the other way around. Your mind is still coming to perfection, it is similar to downloading a large file on a computer to perform an upgrade. The upgrade is going on in your mind, unpacking the deeper truths of the universe. Which I bet you can understand how large in scale this behemoth must be. It will continue to unload on your mind as you learn more, but the initial upgrade will be hardest for the next few years since there is a lot you need to catch up on. Your mind may be susceptible to psychological attacks during this time."

Even the information James presented to me was difficult to digest. I laid down on the bed and James brought over some ice. It was as if he knew my needs before I could say anything by doing the things he did to attend to me. He truly was the great physician. As I rested, I could overhear bits and pieces of the discussion Dillie and James had with one another. There was a lot of discussion about what was happening with the Martians. Listening to them caused my mind to race through my newfound knowledge. My head started throbbing so I slowed my breath to strong, steady inhales and exhales. The pain came in waves. I moved around a lot of information, defragmenting my mind in a sense. I did not have a lot of thought space for other things, so I needed to let it work. As my mind sorted my thoughts into a coherent picture, I began to understand. "Fenie!" I shouted it as loud as I could, startling the two Martian fugitives in my room. "The secret to life; plants, fruits, or fish is Fenie. I was thinking about it, but I could not figure it out because I was unpacking all of the information from the download. But now my mind is clear and I can see."

The reaction of wonder in the faces of Dillie and James made me proud to have figured it out first, but also self-conscious that I might have got it wrong. James opened his mouth to speak first, "Impossible. Someone would have needed to harvest Fenie in a state fit for mass consumption and give it to us without us realizing until it was too late."

His sentence resonated in my mind with such ease. The circumstances were so familiar as if I knew it myself, but needed a reminder. I paused in wonder of the power of this ancient knowledge. New information was steadily unpacking, going into the agricultural aspects of Fenie and the history of its cultivation. I stopped myself from digging any further and focused my mind on the issue. I discerned the possibilities and settled on one, "The secret to life; plants, fruits, or fish. It is not one, but all three. There is a double riddle. Fenie is the secret to life on Mars. Water is the secret to life on Earth. The Fenie has an oil component that can be extracted and dumped in the water supply. The oil would infect the plants and fruits because they were being tended with water in the gardens. Fish are imported, but placed in the water containers saturated with Fenie oil."

James yelped with glee and ran over to shake my hand. "How magnificent, exhibiting this level of discernment and managing to control the unloading of information. Most Martians require years before the flow slows down."

As James continued on his monologue of excitement at my skills, going as far as to suggest human trials, I sat back down to process further. "The saboteur; an heir to the throne. Removing the joint; angels never known." The other Martians stopped jabbering and looked over to me. I did not want to ruin the good that came out of us figuring this one part of the quest, but I knew that I needed to do more. This mystery was not finished. However, my mind was heavy from all of the work I had put it through. I was a human and limited in my ability to operate without rest. "Sleep," I spurted, "I am going to sleep for an hour. We can continue the conversation after I get up. Dillie ran over to me as I collapsed and she helped me into bed. I was able to rest easier in the company of my new friends.

Chapter 22

I woke up one hour later from my rest and fell prone to the floor into a meditative state. It was an automatic response as I pondered the futility of satisfaction in what my eyes could see. I lamented over the time I spent worrying about things that did not live beyond the season they were created for. Such restoration rushed through my body that I was surprised I did not do this instead of sleeping.

As I rose from my state, I realized Dillie and James were no longer in the room with me. My mind nudged me, pointing me to a conversation they had as I slept. I could hear the echoes of their words as if reliving the moment. Dillie and James were going to find a Martian named John. John was the key to something and it involved him meeting me. They were careful with their word choice as if they knew my subconscious mind was listening. I wondered what power I had been given. It felt so good and I could sense I had the authority to control the physical world around me. I was about to reach my hand out to see whether I had telekinetic powers, when a voice reached from inside telling me "It is a gift, not yours to test." Laying my hand back to my side, I trusted the voice and prepared for my day.

And then a knock came to the door. I opened it without hesitation to a waiting Lily. She ran inside and slammed the door shut. I was shocked, but pleased to see her. She warmed my heart every time I came into her presence. I wanted to hug her, but I let the moment pass.

"Joseph," she said in such a way that my insides fluttered. "I read this book all night. Just stayed up reading, no food, no sleep." She collapsed into my arms and I held her. I wrapped my arms around her and laid her on my bed. Temptation demanded I lay next to her, but I resisted and sat at the foot of the bed. "Resistance, just read it."

I felt an urge and touched her forehead. Something released from inside of me and she closed her eyes. A voice deep inside reassured me that she would wake completely refreshed within an hour. In the meantime, I began reading.

As the book unfolded page by page, my mind unfolded ancient understandings and deeper truths about the Martian exploration of Earth. Previous generations of Martians had come to Earth. Hughneirs, to be specific, and then another thought entered my mind. The Hughneirs and their history. A big three that governed the Martian society as a whole: the technology Hughneir, the Great Cultivator; the health Hughneir, the Great Physician; and the societal Hughneir, the Mediating Judge. Dillie was the obvious candidate for the Great Cultivator, it became clear when she sold the knowledge. I wondered why she was never referred to by her title. James called himself the Great Physician, but he was not involved at the compound. Were Martians familiar with those terms? I asked the question to generate deeper searching of my mind, but could not uncover a reason for the gap.

The book proved useful in shedding light on humanity, circa 1500 A.D. Abalam Shaduam, a Mediating Judge from a few generations prior absconded from the Martian planet on a secret mission to scout other planets suitable for habitation. He postulated the rapid fall of Mars due to a deterioration of the Martian mind. On Earth, Abalam toured every continent, spending years observing humanity. His conclusion to never consider Earth was a result of witnessing "A true mental poison, that infects all who contact them." He wrote of meeting another being. This was, by far, the most disturbing accounts and he left Earth, shaken up from the experience. The passage read:

June 6

I woke up this morning to a man standing over me. He told me to rise and we walked to the top of a mountain. Overlooking the plains of the jungle, this man's countenance changed to the most sinister look I have ever seen. I was looking into the face of the poison, but I was more surprised about the human not being stunned by my existence. It was as if the man expected me. The beast began to speak, it was not human and identified itself as the Master of this world. Things around me shifted and the ground shook. The power this being had was ancient. It warned me to leave its humans alone and demanded that I never bring Dworeans to this place.

Reading that story brought shivers to my spine and made me wonder how close I had come to this Master. Was Fien the master? *He could not be,* my internal monologue responded back and brought up memories of Fien mentioning his employer. The master of this world presented a difficult concept in my mind about what I would do if I ever faced it.

Lily sprung into action almost as soon as she awoke from her slumber. "Did you read it?" She appeared well rested, but I was more impressed with her ability to rise, ready for work.

"Yes, I tapped ancient knowledge and my own experiences to understand what we are up against." I looked again to Lily. "I met with my father." I could barely spit out the word before Lily reached out and embraced me. She held me tight and we lingered there for much longer than I imagined I would need her to hold me. It felt good to be held by Lily.

"I am so sorry you had to find out this way, Joseph. You asked me for Josiah's address and I was not sure what he did or did not know. The message did not need to come from me."

I accepted her assessment of the sensitivity. "The news of Josiah not being my biological father was not unwelcome. I was not impressed with him despite the changes he made in his life." I laughed at the thought of spending my whole life looking up to a man who was not my father. Relief swept over me and had us both stuck in a nervous chuckle about the next question.

Lily did me a favor by breaking the chuckling and answering my next question. "Well, you must be wondering who is your real father and if he is from Dworea. I have tested your blood and it is true that you have genetic sequencing suggesting Dworean heritage. So I think your father is Dworean and I have a specific being in mind. Around the time you were born, a Dworean had escaped from the custody of Area 51 guards and was never heard from again. His name is John Hart."

My heart stopped and my mind went back to James and Dillie's conversation. I discussed my meeting with Dillie and James. Lily seemed disturbed that James was still around, informing me that Jacob had assumed James's duties. She told me that those three were the most important Dworeans to humanity because they held incredible amounts of information and power. Lily also explained that I was not a Mediating Judge for the Dworeans like John was, but the way genes transfer in humans makes sense that I would carry John's dominant gifts.

I could not believe what I was hearing. My father was a Martian, the Mediating Judge of the Martians. I rejoiced inside at the possibilities of being able to unite with him and ask him questions about my mother. Lily reminded me that John may not be father material, hence he was never around and Martians were more of a communal society. Despite that reminder, I anticipated a meeting with the being I could refer to as father.

Lily urged discretion, which I corroborated. I realized my status would make me valuable to both the humans and Martians. My safety was a concern because I would be tested if caught and neither set of beings may accept my status with their fold. I was one of a kind, and that reality burrowed deep into my mind. No one else in the universe was like me and could know what I was going through.

Then, I felt a nudge as if something prompted in my mind to continue the work at hand. It began asking questions and looking into her heart. I had to ask, "You could have called me, why did you come to my hotel?"

Lily looked at me and smiled. "Your power of discernment is becoming an unrelenting force. I am shocked at how well you have adapted yourself to the Martian gift. The makings of a leader in human society seem to be your next station in life." With that she sighed and told me her tale of events after I left. Word spread among the Martians that Dillie had departed. This caused speculation about whether Lily had something to do with it and the beings began saying that Dillie had fled for her life. With other Martians becoming sick due to the epidemic, the healthy ones assumed Lily was involved in the treachery. Lily was the one to secretly take over the Martian compound in America, hoisted the good of the entire Martian species as well as blame on her shoulders. They distrusted her even further because the beings observed how she was affiliated with me and concluded she was working with the humans to destroy Martians. A mob of humans formed outside, protesting the Martians' presence because of the sickness that was affecting them. She needed a place to hide and thought of me. "It is all over the television." She turned it on.

We watched for a few minutes as the anchors on the TV speculated and political pundits gossiped about what was causing the Martians to be sick. They argued about whether or not it was contagious and how it may affect humans. Martians were arrested and their possessions seized all over the world. There was talk of placing them back in Area 51 until the technology could be harnessed to send them home. "Anywhere but here on Earth," cried the President of the United States. "I have talked with other world leaders and they have placed similar restrictions on the Martians." On other channels, there was talk of biological warfare and mass genocide. I sat disgusted at humanity over the widespread hate. The Martians needed help, not destruction. I calmed myself down and searched my mind for answers, the only answer. "The Master of Earth."

Lily looked at me confused. "The Master of Earth from the book? Do you think it was true or some sort of imagery?"

I was surprised at Lily for her lack of faith in Abalam Shaduam's work, but I accepted that she had not seen the sort of things I saw. I explained the interactions with Fien in more detail, hoping that would open her eyes. We finished the conversation to a long pause when we looked at the TV to see Martians, naked, in cages with numbers etched to wooden boards and tied around their necks. I felt a deep pain inside and wept until Lily came over to comfort me. My soul ached for those beings and the hatred of humanity over something that was not well understood. Lily wept with me as well and I felt a strong connection to her soul as a result. It was at that moment that I realized I loved her. She was my heart and soul, and I needed her to hold me.

I composed myself and broke the silence. "We must get back to the compound. Lily, your fellow beings need you and I will try to reach the hearts of my fellow man." A fear crept its way into my heart and I knew I needed to embrace this mission even if it may cost me my life.

Lily nodded, and we began packing up to head back to the compound. I wondered where Dillie and James went, but I had to focus myself on other priorities. On the way back to the compound, we saw numerous police vehicles corralling a large crowd of people. They were so busy that they did not notice Lily and me riding past them. We wove onto back roads and made our way to a secret entrance to the Martian compound.

The Martians were not pleased to see Lily and me walking down the hallways. An announcement was made for the Martians to assemble in the cafeteria where Lily would address them all. I concerned myself with Lily's wellbeing, because she seemed more drained now than before she fell asleep. We walked into a room full of silent Martians as Lily prepared to address them.

Chapter 23

The Martians gathered in the cafeteria. The setting was a makeshift stage with two chairs and a single podium. As Lily walked into the room, the air felt heavy with unresolved tension. Martians looked to her: some smiling, some grimacing, and rest uncertain. She walked into the room with her head held high by herself and up to the stage. I stood by the door, preparing myself to carry out my part of the plan, address all of humanity. But first, to hear her speech.

Another Martian walked from the crowd and up on the stage. Well dressed and intellectual, like Lily. They seemed a perfect match and my jealousy threatened to bubble up. Lily looked to her fellow being an asked, "Well Jacob, shall I go first or you?" They caucused for a moment and then Jacob emerged to the podium as Lily took her seat.

"My fellow Martians," Jacob began. "We have been betrayed by our very own. Lily has come before us to assume supreme leadership for your well-being." I could tell the accusation annoyed Lily somewhat. In my heart, I whispered a prayer for her to not be consumed with anger. She settled down back to her relaxed state. "Lily has ousted our leader, Dillie, and inserted herself as leader through a private ceremony. Conspiring with a human, Lily has advanced her personal agenda to rob the Martians of our inheritance and undermine our chances at getting back home. Lily wants to stay with the humans and fuel her lust for greed and power."

The room shook with the collective outrage of the Martians. My senses began to overwhelm me with confusion and pain from the beings in the room. All of the beings, even

Lily, except for one, Jacob. He was not hurting, I could tell because I could sense his heart and it lacked a true pain. I started searching my mind again. Something about him reminded me of Dillie.

"We must protect ourselves from this monster who is not aligned with us." He slammed his hand against the podium. The room of Martians nodded their heads in agreement. "Getting with humans and committing all sorts of indecency."

I scoffed, but straightened up when the Martians directed varied shushes at me. Jacob continued his diatribe against Lily for another thirty minutes, presenting multiple points and sub-points to dignify his argument. He talked of priorities and the illness and discussed how he would like to see democratic elections for the Martians. The room erupted into shock and multiple discussions. The crowd turned against him and Lily sat smug in her chair as she waited her turn. I swore she knew this was going to happen. With that controversial statement, the crowd demanded Lily to come forward and rejected the argument from Jacob. He took his seat.

Lily moved toward the stage as the crowd shouted questions at her like, "Are these allegations true? Are you in league with the Human?" Lily raised her hands and began to talk to her people. "The rift between humanity and Martians has grown exponentially in recent years. Ask any two humans about Martian rights and one will find a spectrum of opinions and emotions, some rooted in well-thought arguments and others based on group think. When it comes to being a Martian, we are in the position of waiting for the litigation of humanity's laws in humanity's world. We had the technology to take them out years ago, but that is inconsistent with our tenets."

I reacted with surprise to that statement, but my mind drifted to the technology of Martians when they came to Earth. I realized how much power the Martians held in their technology and how well they had masked such power. I was more impressed with Dillie for balancing the flow of information to the humans about Martian technology without giving them the ability for grave destruction. All of the technology and all of the information in the world today was influenced in some way by Martian technology.

They debated back and forth for some time with one another. The points and counterpoints shot back and forth between Lily and her rival. Each statement from their lips suggested rehearsal with well-timed phrases, even their body language was a careful action to give upper hand. I wondered if other Martians knew this or if this was just something I observed because of human politics. My mind woke up again to remind me that it was both. As if from a voice from behind, I heard my knowledge inform me that Martians were ascended beyond humanity, but not all have the ability to discern. That was a specific gift, like other gifts for Martians. My gift of discernment, combined with my understanding of human mannerisms, helped me know these things. I smiled to myself for this knowledge as if I had a secret. My mind replied to my musings, "be humble."

The debate concluded and the room fell silent. I sensed a change in the air, like the realization that a choice would have to be made. The division among the beings was evident, with Martians separating from one another with looks of disgust. They sat in circles of like-minded creatures and struggled to consensus over a clear leader. I waved to the stage and got Lily's attention for us to meet in another room. She pointed towards the kitchen and I walked that way. Once in the kitchen, I looked around, a little surprised that I beat her to the kitchen.

Then the door opened. "Joseph, I am sorry, but Jacob insisted on coming in as well." Lily's agitation made me feel honored that she would rather be alone with me than to have Jacob in the room as well. It also made me suspicious of Jacob's intentions for Lily.

My question to Jacob came off with aggravation as well. "What are you doing here?" I felt bad for showing my annoyance, but it was hard for me to resist because I felt he was my rival.

"I want to be here in case you two are plotting against me. I plan to implement a transparent process with you two gone. Lily, you have betrayed your species by being in leagues with this human. We are a numbered species and you are one of the best available Martians. I am working insane hours to rid us of this plague and it is astounding that you find this human more appealing than you own." Jacob huffed at the end of his monologue and crossed his arms. Listening to Jacob made me realize how appealing Lily was to the Martians and caused me to wonder how she was perceived among them for colluding with me.

"Dr. Ryemore, I am glad you bring up your medical service. Although your work on our dying species has been beneficial. It has only provided marginal benefits, and you have been holding back." The silence in the room after Lily's statement lingered for a few moments as Jacob's slack jaw could not find its way back to his upper lip. "I have been paying attention Doctor Ryemore. While you have not allowed Martians to die yet, I have news that you know of a remedy that will heal us, but you are taking a longer time to 'test' it."

My mind started racing, 'The souls of many; away like a mist. The secret to life; plants, fruits, or fish. The saboteur; an heir to the throne. Removing the joint; angels never known. The saboteur; an heir to the throne. Removing the joint; angels never known.' Jacob babbled, "Well yes, Lily, but research this sensitive..."

"Stop!" I shouted with all of my authority and they both fell silent with their eyes glued to me. "The saboteur; an heir to the throne. Removing the joint; angels never known." I repeated the phrase as I walked toward's Jacob. I was beyond annoyance and boiling with rage. I felt the anger of the collective beings and wanted to punish Jacob for his sins. "You are a doctor?" It was not a question, but he nodded as he looked into my eyes with fear. My senses weakened with my rage, but I could tell he was lamenting. And then a flash of realization landed on my mind. I saw inside his heart the sense of entitlement for his post. "You believe you are next in line for the role of Great Physician? The saboteur; an heir to the throne." He backed away while holding his hands up to explain, but I did not need any more explanation. I took the rest in my own hand. "Removing the joint; angels never known. A parallel to another Jacob with true ambition. You feel it is your birthright." I grabbed Jacob's arm. "You stand accused Dr. Ryemore, tell me of your diabolical plan and subsequent collusion with Fien."

His eyes widened with great fear and I calmed down as I realized what I was doing to him. My mind slowed and opened up to me more. I sensed that it was not quite correct. "I am so sorry." Jacob ripped his shirt and confessed his sins. "You are right about everything. You have told me so much about myself. I am wrong and I know it. I received a message to meet a man outside the compound, his name was Fien. This man offered me the cure for Martians sickness, as long as I told him about Martian biology. So I complied. I wanted to become the next leader of my fellow beings." I was shocked at this revelation, but Jacob revealed that he never betrayed his fellow beings. He divulged biological information because he knew that it would not aid the humans in biological warfare. The reason Martians were getting sick was because of them showing symptoms of becoming fallen. He knew their time on Earth would have to be limited and pushed of separation as much as possible to prevent contamination with humanity's sickness.

Jacob looked to me. "I could sense you knew what was inside my mind. What are you?" I did not understand the question, and gave him only a shrug. Lily looked to us, but I could tell this was overwhelming for her to see. I lamented becoming so angry at Jacob and the obvious manipulation from Fien. The realization hit me that my work was not finished and the real war was only about to begin.

I looked to Jacob and Lily, and offered, "Do not take Dillie's approach. You both have qualities that would lend to a cooperative leadership." I ran outside to stop humanity.

Chapter 24

I made my way to the rusted gates where the boundary between humanity and Martians existed. The wall was a division in so many ways, not just in location. The crowd swelled and packed as I walked to the podium. My hands shook and my teeth rattled, giving away the pent-up nervousness inside.

The national guard had formed a wall, symbolic of the war that had been waged with words. I looked to the sky, late afternoon, a beautiful sunset that could have been better suited for an evening with Lily. Sniffing the air, I accepted what may come of me. I was willing to accept whatever treatment the humans gave if it meant I was doing the right thing. The anger in the air was strong, hatred overwhelmed my senses of these people.

I stood at the podium. It was a little too tall for me and I had to set myself on my tip toes so I could reach the microphone. I placed my shaking hands on the podium to still them and that sufficed to still the ever-growing crowd.

"Friends," I began with a slight break in my voice. "I am here today to ask what troubles you. I look out and I see men and women with torches, guns, knives, and other accouterments of war. Have we learned nothing over the years?" The people began looking around at each other. My hope was that they would see what they were doing and put away their weapons.

I waited for eyes to make their way back to me. "Maybe I should applaud you for this behavior. Never before have I seen so much unity among Americans as to see white people, black people, Asian people, and many other races of humans join together for such a cause. Just thirty years ago, we were in the dark. We had no idea about extraterrestrial life and we were all fighting wars against each other over our limited resources." A nerve was struck, I sensed the hearts of man being turned from stone to cream. They were accepting what I was saying. I felt a sense of accomplishment of being able to help them understand.

"Now look at us," this was where the sting would come. "We are so educated and so privileged. The same people who assumed we were the only ones in the universe, just some 30 years ago. The same beings we enslaved and reaped the benefits from since the mid-1900s, we are now going to show up to their front door and make demands? They should make demands, they were the ones who were wronged. Yet we scooped up their fellow beings and locked them in cages like dogs. We are the monsters, the animals, the criminals, the bad guys. Not them. Us."

The crowd began to put down their defenses. I could feel the peace being restored and the healing in the hearts. Except for one part. One part of the crowd was burning hotter than any hate I could imagine. It was a hate that needed to be weeded out and burned. And then I saw him, Fien. He was standing behind a man with a poster that read, 'Martians will burn in Hell.' The man was not spectacular and did not express any ill will, but Fien grabbed his shoulder. The wicked smile on the monster's face was the most inhuman I have ever seen. I started running towards the crowd to catch him, and then the man erupted in a hateful tirade against Martians. The anger spread through the crowd like a plague of epic proportions and they began to spit at me and throw things at me.

I stayed focused on Fien. In the crowd, I was being hit from all places. the pain was unbearable, but I had to catch up to him. These people were being influenced by this man, and I had to stop him. My consciousness began to fade as it struggled to keep up with my opponent who was sauntering towards a nearby warehouse. He looked back and smiled at me with his wicked look. The people beat on me further, "Not me, get him." I shouted the words, but it was like they did not see him. Something hard hit my head and I fell down, seeing black.

And then a hand grabbed my shoulder and pulled me back into life. I had given up, laying there to accept my fate. "I am not that strong, so you are going to have to pull yourself up." Bonnie's voice sprung me into action and I lifted up again to walk to the warehouse. The people now made a path. I marveled at her level of influence to get the people to follow her lead. We made it to the door without any more disruptions and entered the large metal door.

It closed behind us and Bonnie let me go. I fell to the ground with a thud. "Be gentle," I chided her, but no one was behind me. "Where did you go?" I shouted but there was nowhere to go except through a door on the far side of the room.

Then the door opened and it walked into the room. An air of superiority, as if it was in charge of the world, was around us. It twisted a smirk onto Bonnie's face, but this was not Bonnie. The way in which it carried itself was distinct from Bonnie. I could tell because Bonnie walked with confidence, but would seem off balance when in heels. This Bonnie glided on the ground as if the floor was ice. The master of this world walked with more authority.

The oppressiveness in the room felt like a dark, ominous shadow that hovered over my person. Much like the experience of spilling flour on oneself, I felt a presence that would not be easily shaken. I experienced discomfort.

"Joseph, I sense the great power that resides inside. It is almost impossible for me to coexist in this room with you." It caressed its hands up Bonnie's frame. "A vessel, as you can tell. But I had to see you, I had heard so much."

The voice sounded like the flowing of ocean current. The etiquette, the respect, the flattery, and yet I felt so offended hearing her voice. My inner sense of righteousness demanded I respond in anger. I felt myself starting to hate the person in front of me. But then I went back to that secret place in my mind. I dwelled there for moment and delighted in the lovely thoughts of peaceful coexistence between the beings. The destructive thoughts departed as quickly as they arrived.

"What do you want, adversary?"

Bonnie kept circling me, and I tried to keep her in front of me.

"Astute, I see. Your predecessors have never identified me this quickly. Maybe this is because you are unlike any of my opponents before."

Its opponents before? I knew of the Martian that had traveled to Earth many centuries ago but I did not know of any others. My mind allowed me to drift to the possibility of human judges. How many judges had existed on Earth and why were there not anymore? What happened to humanity so that we would lose our judges? Am I a judge? Was I a mistake? Should you exist? Why were you betraying humanity? The Martians were the real enemy. You lust after that Martian. Why would you torment this innocent woman before you?

I began to feel a bit overwhelmed in the moment. And I could not stop my mind from moving. It kept going from topic to topic to topic without allowing me a moment's refuge. Each one like a small incision in my skull. Each one pecking away at my mind, accusing me of sins I never committed. The voices yelled louder. They were screaming at me. My hands began shaking and great drops of sweat populated on my head. I was tempted to close my eyes and rest, but I needed to re-engage my adversary. I lashed out against my thoughts, examining each unhelpful and negative thought to lock deep in my subconscious until I could address them logically. I refused the bait and repeated my original question with more authority. "Cut it out! What do you want, adversary?"

And then the voices stopped. The being looked surprised and irritated at my question. "Interesting, I was certain that my most loyal Fien was mistaken on your power, but seeing it for myself has left me almost feeling sorry for my dearest wormwood. How is it that you came to exist? Ah, an illicit union? Shall I break down the circumstances that led to your existence? No, I shall not. You know already? Your father told you? I lost control over him when he turned his heart over to the God of this universe. But that is..."

I held my right hand up, cutting the master of this world off. "What sort of clairvoyance or witchcraft are you employing?" Feeling more in control of the conversation, I wondered if I had gained the upper hand.

"Clairvoyance? Witchcraft?" The being cackled at my question, a shrieking laugh that could shock a tired room full of people awake. It slapped its knee and doubled over in a giggling delight.

I was beginning to feel self-conscious. The voices started whispering lightly but I recognized its trick before the voices could get louder. "I demand you answer me, adversary." My voice carried with more authority this time. I decided not to allow my arrogance to cloud my thoughts.

The being stood up straight at my words. "None of that, it's a predictive science more or less. I have lived on this earth almost as long as it has existed. Nothing about humanity's mindset surprises me, and I have expert influence over the masses. Also, my subordinates are stationed all over the world and report to me regularly the comings and goings of you."

I was interested to hear more. A being so old, I wanted to know how old. All the thoughts processing through my head were questions on the origin of the universe and life on Earth before recorded history. Were historical recorded events real or fabricated? I felt a tingling sensation in my spine as I imagined all of the possibilities. The interview of an eternity. The world would recognize my resourcefulness and You would receive glory for generations to come. These are not my thoughts. I had to resist again. I broke through the attack. "What do you want, beast? You are not permitted to speak unless to answer my question."

Bonnie's body began sweating and she looked unwell. The being's hold on her was waning and I could tell it was upsetting to the being. "The end is near. I want what you want Joseph. The liberation of the Martians. Martians and humans cannot coexist because of the humans' fallen state. So Martians need to leave, and I can facilitate that."

I thought about what Lily said, and how much she emphasized humanity's unwillingness to work with them.

What would this mean if they could leave Earth? Lily crossed my mind again; would I want her to leave?

The adversary, sensing my musings, said, "This would be a good thing Joseph. Martians would be able to live out their existences consistent with their beliefs and a sense of peace. No humans to destroy their habitat and safety."

I did not believe this being. I could not quite figure out why. This creature was a liar but I could not stop myself from asking, "How would you do it?"

Its face lit up a little, "I have the knowledge and understanding of millennia. Generation after generation have come and gone, but I still live. I have seen the extent of the heavens and the bowels of the earth. I know the origins of all. I can give the Martians my knowledge of coordinated, long range space travel to find a suitable new home or of refitting their current home with the necessary infrastructure to support life. Under my care, they will surely not die."

The grandiose manner in which the being presented its plan impressed me to belief that it could accomplish these things. I left the thought with that point, afraid to allow myself anytime to dwell on it unless my adversary tempted me with its tricks. "Why have you not done it already?"

The being sighed and looked at the floor. I assumed it was feigning humility or nervousness. "Because I am bound to Earth, I would need a piece of their essence. But I cannot reach them due to their nature. I would need some of yours. Once I have their essence, I would be able to influence their nature and give them the tools they needed."

I heard what it said but I was confused. "How would you get some of my nature?"

"A submission to me. You could bow to me or something like that. In return, I will give you dominion over the earth." My reaction must have indicated to the being my unwillingness to something like that as it offered an alternative. "I can also make it very pleasant for you, if you prefer." With that, the being started unbuttoning Bonnie's blouse, revealing her breasts.

I turned my head away from it. "This is not Bonnie and I would not do something like that to her. Please put on your clothes."

I remained facing the other way as I felt hands on my shoulders and her soft body on my back. The voices started shouting in my ears. Each word snarled and bit my conscience, "Do it, you want to, give in, she's beautiful, it is just a little bit, it will be our little secret." The voices became so loud that I placed my hands over my ears. I began shaking and started to cry. I went back to that place where peace reigned. The place where my thoughts were my own. "Think on those things that have virtue and praise." I shouted those words over and over as the voices lowered. I turned and looked the beast in the eye. "My care and attention is to Bonnie alone, not you, creature! Whatever you have planned for the Martians, let it be known that I know it is no good and I will not be a part of it. You have lost this battle and I demand you depart from me."

I felt the tension shift in the room to the space behind me. I knew the monster was on its last leg. "Very well, I cannot take any more. But please, I beg of you to send me back home. If you do not specify, I can be banished into the deepest part of Earth, never to return."

"Why should I care? Answer me quickly." I remained facing the wall away from Bonnie. I wanted to keep my advantage.

"There is a war going on that is older than you can imagine. I am but a pawn in a much larger scheme. I will leave this place and prowl for other human subjects."

I considered its offer. I could rid the world of one of its adversaries, but I knew my limitations. There could be a much larger war going on that could create chaos where there was none. I also considered that the beast was lying and could launch another attack when I tried to challenge it. I was tired and wanted to rest. "You have my leave to do what you must. Go away."

Bonnie's body jerked, but not before she released a howl that burned my brain. She also scratched her body in repeated patterns until welts appeared. I attempted to intervene, but then a peace settled over the room a moment later. Then, the shouts of many on the outside. As if their souls were being ripped from their bodies. I assume the people outside were no longer being controlled. A terrible feeling washed over me as I sensed the people scratching their bodies raw and screeching their voices hoarse from pain.

I took a deep breath and turned around to a frightened Bonnie Wrait, who was now covered up. Her voice shook and her teeth chattered between words when she said, "I...I...I am so...so sorry, I had no control. But what are you? Are you God?"

I was tempted to laugh at that question until I realized that she was a witness to the events but did not have any control. It must have terrified her to see this happen. I walked towards her, reaching out my hand to touch her shoulder. She stumbled backwards trying to get away from me. I felt bad for her in the moment. I wondered what reaction a human would give the real God. "I am not God Bonnie. I am a human with a Martian essence. You have been through a lot. Please do not be afraid, I am not going to harm you."

She stayed against the wall but she stopped trembling at my words. "What happened to me?"

I thought for a moment and considered explaining how judges and spirits worked in this world. However, I knew she would not be ready for that. I felt that she deserved to know, but I doubted she could handle the truth in that her mental disposition, along with her warped worldview probably allowed the master of the universe to make a connection. It made things worse for her because of the strangeness of our relationship. "There are beings in this world that are more powerful than you can imagine. They prey on humans in order to gain control of their bodies because they lack one of their own. You probably were having nightmares and stressful attacks for weeks before you were taken over."

She nodded her head, her facial expression got more serious. "What can I do to protect myself in the future?"

I sighed. "Nothing you can do except turn away from your hatred of the Martians. That was the most powerful and cunning being I have ever encountered. Providing a challenge to it would require self-denial through fasting or praying. Just trust in the God of the universe to see you through."

Bonnie stood up slowly. She looked like she had not slept in some time. Her face showed signs of bruising, probably due to the foreign body inside of her and the way it forced her muscles in her face to move. I thought to myself how terrible she looked and her face made me a little sick. Bonnie said, "What should I do now?"

"You should change your life. Go find out what it means to love others the way you love yourself. Embrace the Martians and work for their deliverance."

She nodded her head again. She turned to walk out of the door but turned back and ran over to hug me. This hug felt genuine, like she appreciated what I had done. I wondered how embarrassed she must have felt at all of this. Contemplating the power of the adversary, I wondered how powerful it would be if I had given in to its request. I imagined that it would eventually have made a mess of the Martians, as it seemed to have done to humanity. I wondered if its strategy would have changed from the beginning. Walking home, I felt exhausted, but also felt a strong power growing inside of me. I had a growing sense of confidence and a sight of the world that most others would never see. I counted my blessings and estimated how far I could have pushed for answers. As I fell asleep back at the compound, I wondered what it must have been like in the earth's garden before the adversary showed up.

Chapter 25

Waking up at the compound felt more familiar than any other place in the world. It could have been my exhaustion from the night before, but my respite was rejuvenating. I rose to breathe in the fresh aroma and came at face level with Dillie.

"You know you were in a deep sleep? I tried rousing you on multiple occasions for the past two hours." She rocked back and forth in place, much like a lunatic would, or maybe a baby. Dillie had lost the ability to force a reaction out of me and I just sat there looking at her, uninterested. She stopped rocking and got up to walk out of the room.

Before the door could close behind her, it opened again. Half expecting one of Dillie's tricks, I shouted, "No thank you Dillie. That is about all I can handle today." Only it was not Dillie. Another Martian that I did not recognize walked into the room and sat in the chair which was facing me. He looked around the same age as Dillie and James. I was not certain, but there were only a handful of Martians who were as old as the Great Cultivator and the Great Physician. Considering this particular Martian was coming to see me, I assumed he was— "John Hart, the Mediating Judge. Welcome sir." I nodded by head in a half bow, hand to my chest, to offer my respect.

"Even though you are not Martian, your recognition of my past stature and our sacred traditions is the sincerest form of flattery I can receive. You may call me Eonayanaa. Thank you." He was well-spoken and seemed more relaxed than his peers. He spoke with a deep whisper, even paced, pleasant to hear and relaxing to me somewhat. We both sat looking at one another. The question hung in the air like a dense steam at a spa. "I heard word that a human was here and that we have a genetic connection. Is your mother Angeline Babbit?"

There it was, the words spit out of his mouth with the eloquence of a toddler who has not known shame. The father I never knew was staring me in the face and asked me if I was my mother's son. Then the fear came. I could feel the doubt swell in my mind like a bruise on my brain left no space in my skull. The voice rang like the pounding of tiny hammers inside of my mind. I needed to compose myself; I responded to his question with a simple answer.

"Yes."

The fear receded.

"Joseph. Please forgive me, my son." The being, my father, stood and fell to the floor with a bow, my mind reminding me this was a symbol of repentance for the Martians. I reached my hand down to his shoulder and he rose back to my level. We embraced, and all things felt right in my mind. "I have wondered about and looked for Angeline for years. How is she doing?"

"She passed some years ago to pneumonia. Mom was always hard on herself, and sort of lost the will to live once I went off to college." Reflecting back on her demise resurrected a sense of pain in my heart like no other. I forgot how much losing her had caused me grief. Eonayanaa reached out and patted my shoulder to tell me it was okay.

We talked for hours as he told me about the Angeline he knew. Neither one of us knew the truth about how a Martian and a human could reproduce an offspring. Eonayanaa chalked up the possibility to their compatible state of minds. He said, "We were both prisoners. I was stuck in Area 51 and she with Josiah." My father made my mother sound like a princess because he was so favorable towards her in his memory. John indicated that his 'indiscretion' with Angeline caused him to lose his gift to discern, so he declined to rejoin the Martian fold once freedom was granted. Distraught, my father traveled to the ends of the earth seeking out the deeper truths within the world. There he discovered the extent of his fallen nature. The longer Martians stayed on Earth, the more the cares of this world dominated their minds. My heart rejoiced at the realization that my real father was much more interesting than my mind conjured him up to be.

I told Eonayanaa of my childhood and my genetic reception of Martian abilities. Talking on my mother's relationship with my father, I admitted my lack of understanding until a recent discussion with Josiah. The happiness my mother experienced after Josiah left could not be understated. My father sat and listened, soaking in every detail about my mother's life. I wondered whether he still loved her.

Eonayanaa and I built a bond of unbreakable strength in the time we spent together. He was the father I never knew and he seemed so easy to know.

I divulged to him my deepest secrets, including details on my love for Lily. He offered me the support of a father, but cautioned me that continuing on with one another would disqualify her from leading the Martians. Being with me would cause Lily to be questioned as a leader, by both the humans and Martians. As I was one of my kind, John told me that it may be more appropriate to remain single until we could understand if there were others and how beings like me came into existence. I accepted his advice but I knew in my mind that I would be with Lily if that was what she wanted.

We emerged from my room to find a small committee of Dillie, James, Jacob, and Lily standing outside my door. They received me with open arms and offered me asylum with them. Because of my gift as Mediating Judge, I had the duty to bestow the gifts upon the new Hughneirs, Jacob and Lily. I blessed them and laid my hands to recognize them as leaders in a private ceremony. Lily became the Great Cultivator and Jacob, the Great Physician.

Dillie said, "Congrats to the official leaders of the Martians! We will have a public ceremony for the benefit of the Martians to demonstrate our unity." Dillie looked to me. "We cannot recognize you as a Hughneir, but I ask that you remain available for the day we select a new Mediating Judge. It may take years, and you can have my home."

I was honored but a bit surprised. Everyone was supportive and told me that I could remain as long as I wanted. Selecting a new Mediating Judge could take multiple decades, as the gift associated with a Judge was rare. I considered how old I would be and what would be my ultimate age when it would all end.

I decided to leave the Martian compound anyway and find my true calling. Packing up my things, I reflected on everything that had happened. Why did Dillie choose to make all of those decisions regarding selling Martian technological secrets by herself? Why not figure out a solution that would work for the board members as opposed to taking a check and building communities with little value? I won't lie, I thought her motivations may have been sinister, but I also believed that she cared for her fellow beings. How that affection turned into an excuse to manipulate the freedom of millions of Martians for her own personal gain was beyond unethical. It seemed as though she would depart after the ceremony and never return.

This was not done in accordance with Martian laws, but I did not feel that was appropriate. I applauded Lily for embracing this resolution, but my ascended understanding reminded me that these trials were not over. This was because Dillie would be a liability and a wildcard as long as she was alive. If she was dead, Lily controlled the story. If Dillie was alive, she would answer for herself and she tended to say and do irrational things. Despite this, Dillie would have to leave.

I also wondered about James and Jacob. I did not know much about either one, but the Martian disease was under control. The Master of this World and Fien gave me a riddle, but they were liars and defeated. Engaging them anymore would prove to be destructive. I cautioned Lily and Jacob to guard their hearts and to call if they ever felt in danger.

As I finished packing, Dillie was jabbering away about what she was going to do in retirement.

"Oh, I am so old, what will I do? Traveling to a different country would be fun. I want to travel to other planets again. I heard the edge of the solar system will be picturesque in the next 10 years."

I could not help but laugh with her. She was definitely happier now that the truth had been revealed. At the back of my mind, I was still cautious, but things were good for a moment. I knew that I needed to take my leave of the Martians for some time. I may have discovered that I was Martian in part, but that was not enough for me. I wanted to understand my purpose and how I was supposed to contribute to the movement. I also needed to reexamine what I valued in life, as Lily had made me think about the possibilities of love.

Just then, Lily knocked on the door. I turned to see her standing in the doorway. She was looking at me and tried to give a smile, but I could tell that it was forced.

Dillie stopped talking and said, "I should give you two some space." Dillie quickly got up and walked out of the room, shutting the door behind her.

Lily looked at me and I stared back at her. No words for what felt like an eternity. We were just standing there, looking at each other.

"You are beautiful," was the only thing I managed to squeak out. I was in love with this woman.

Lily walked up to me, placed her hands on my shoulder, right on top of my collar bones, and passionately kissed me. I held her tightly and she was holding me. We just stood there, enjoying each individual moment.

"I never want this moment to end," I said fighting back tears.

"You and me both," Lily replied, just as emotional.

We finally tore ourselves apart but we were still connected. The energy flowing between us was enough to cause my soul to quake.

"Joseph, as you may know, I do in fact care deeply for you. You are the only being that I know of to cause me to feel this way. I want to give my life to loving you, but I know that I cannot do so with such a responsibility as the one I have inherited from Dillie." She looked down into my chest and was breathing deeply. My hands are wrapped around her waist. "I am so sorry for not seeing things clearer sooner. If I had, maybe we would have been able to build that foundation that could survive the distance that we will have to endure from now on to avoid dissolving our potential union."

I looked at her closely, and I knew she was right. I was just discovering things about myself that had completely changed what I thought about my identity and the truth behind the universe. Lily seemed to be at a loss of words again, and I was about to speak until she said, "Chanselah Arshune, that's my name."

I said, "We will be together Chanselah Arshune, I am sure of it. I promise to keep in touch. I will be back."

She smiled, and looked me in the eyes. She kissed me one more time. "One day, my love, we will see."

Author's Note

Thanks for reading *The Awakening*.

This book took me years to compose and I really appreciate you taking the time to read. I have a few ideas that will come along soon!

For more information on what I currently find interesting and to get updates on my next project, go to www.joneevans.com

About the Author

Jon E. Evans was born in Little Rock, Arkansas and grew up a few miles northwest of Maumelle, Arkansas. Although Jon discovered an interest in books during his childhood, he did not develop an interest in writing until much later in his life. He is an engineer by trade and has developed a number of other interests, including acting, singing, dancing, video games, and sleeping. He loves cheesy science fiction books and thought-provoking classical novels.

Jon is a Christian and loves to debate religious and social topics. His essays, poetry, and a listing of his works in progress are available at www.joneevans.com. It will give readers a look into the paradoxical, and sometimes dark, side of his mind.

Jon lives in the Washington, D.C. Metropolitan area with his wife, Kasi, and they are working to build a life that will pour into others.